THE MASTER OF MARYKNOLL

"*You look a bit lost. Can we help?*"

THE MASTER
OF
MARYKNOLL

By
MALCOLM SAVILLE

with illustrations by
ALICE BUSH

LONDON
EVANS BROTHERS LIMITED

This Evans Centenary edition first published 2008 by
Evans Brothers Limited
2A Portman Mansions
Chiltern Street
London W1U 6NR

British Library Cataloguing in Publication Data
Saville, Malcolm
  The Master of Maryknoll
  1. Adventure stories 2. Children's stories
  I. Title
  823.9'14[J]

ISBN 9780237535711

First published by Evans Brothers Limited 1950

Printed in Great Britain by Mackays of Chatham plc, Chatham, Kent

CONTENTS

ILLUSTRATIONS

FOREWORD

THE adventures described in this story took place soon after the war when everybody in Britain was rationed for things like meat, sweets, butter and petrol. Hardly anybody could afford a new car, and that is why Mr. Buckingham's exciting journey to London by road was so hazardous!

Ludlow and Hereford are real, and you can go there yourself, like Juliet, Simon and Charles—but you may not be able to find the meadow where the Fair was held and neither will you discover the verger's cottage.

So far as I know, there is no common or house called Leasend, but there is a Mary Knowle valley below the woods of High Vinalls. The house which I have called Maryknoll (pronounced Marrynoll) is imaginary, and so are Mr. Septimus Bland and all the other people in this story.

MALCOLM SAVILLE.

Holroyds,
Barcombe,
Lewes,
Sussex.

7

CHAPTER I

CRISIS FOR CHARLES

CHARLES RENISLAU looked considerably older than his fourteen and a half years. He was a trifle thin for his height, and although the lock of black hair which invariably drooped over his right eyebrow was rather unusual for a schoolboy very few people who met him for the first time realized that he was only half English.

Later, when they were told his surname and noticed that he was, perhaps, more excitable than most boys of his age and heard that he was an unusually good musician, most grown-ups regarded his good looks with renewed interest and found it easy enough to believe that he was the son of a Polish composer who had disappeared after the defence of Warsaw in 1939.

Charles, of course, could hardly remember what his father looked like, for he was only four when his mother brought him to England. Alex Renislau was nevertheless a very real person to his son for, almost every day since that nightmare journey of escape, his mother had talked to the boy about his father.

" Never forget, Charles, that your father was a very great composer. If he had decided to share his gifts instead of sacrificing himself for his country his name to-day would be world famous. . . . When he sent us away from Warsaw he knew what was coming and I have never been quite sure whether he loved music or his beloved Poland the most. He was great and brave and honest and you must never forget that you are his only son."

And, to do him justice, Charles never did forget, and although perhaps it was natural enough that he should sometimes take his wonderful mother for granted during the difficult years of the war when he was growing into a schoolboy, the man who was his father and whom he would never see, often seemed to be at his side to help him when help was most needed.

Their only photograph showed the head and shoulders of a slight, clean-shaven man with sensitive eyes and lips —a man who looked strangely young in his uniform. This photograph had been copied several times, but although Charles' portrait of his father was a little blurred he knew every line of the kindly face by heart.

When Mrs. Renislau had landed in England with only two suitcases, a violin and a lively, but bewildered, small boy who was entirely dependent upon her, she was without a home and practically without an income. She had only just said "Good-bye" to her husband whom she might never see again and although her only relative was a brother living in Shropshire, who she knew had been out of sympathy with her marriage, she telephoned to him from London and asked his advice. Martin Strong was a successful business man and although he knew next to nothing about music and was quite unable to understand why anyone should feel compelled to compose it, and was even more amazed that his only sister should choose to marry a musician—and a foreigner at that—he did not hesitate when called upon.

"Catch the 6.10 to Shrewsbury and I'll meet you in the car. Stay at Manlands as long as you wish."

And that was how the only home that Charles knew

was the lovely country house of his uncle—a man whom he had grown to respect but never to love. Manlands was old and big and when after a week or so Mr. Strong had suggested that four rooms on the top floor would make a home for his sister and her boy this seemed to be an excellent arrangement. Charles was too young to know of all his mother went through as the months dragged by without news of his father, and too young to realize what the war meant. Soon he was busy enjoying a new life in the peace of the English countryside, and when, before long, his mother went away every Monday and did not come back to him until Saturday evenings, he could not know that she was doing war-work and trying to make herself independent. Then old Hetty came to look after him, but it was not until years later that he learned that she was his mother's old nurse. After his mother, Hetty was the most wonderful woman he had ever known, for he had never been able to like his Aunt Mary who was cold and snobbish and always suggesting in every possible way that he was inferior to his two cousins, Cyril and Derek, who were one and three years older than himself respectively.

But because the Renislaus had, to some extent, lived apart from the Strongs and because, when he was old enough, Charles had gone daily to the nearest Grammar School four miles away while his cousins had been sent first to an expensive Preparatory School and then on to a Public School, life had been tolerable enough until about three weeks before this story opens, on a July evening—the first of the summer holidays.

Charles was later home on that particular day than usual because there had been a cricket match and, when he was in the mood, Charles enjoyed cricket and was a promising bowler. His mother was waiting for him at the gate of the drive, which she did not often do, and at once he sensed that something was wrong.

"Leave your cycle here, Charles, and come for a walk," she said. " I've got something to tell you."

He was hot, thirsty and longing for his tea, but he dropped his bicycle on the grass and with a choky feeling in his throat turned into the shade of the trees with her and said, " What's wrong, Mother? "

Later, when she had gone away, he tried to remember her actual words but could never really do so. Perhaps she found it difficult to find the words herself, but the sense was clear enough. She was going away without him. To Switzerland. For how long? She didn't know. Why? She couldn't explain now but she would write and he wasn't to worry and everything would be all right. And through all this strange conversation he had the feeling that she was hiding something from him, and never in his life had he felt this before. The shock of this discovery made him almost sulky so that he asked no more questions, and it was not until she had actually left that old Hetty gave him the idea that perhaps she had gone to Switzerland for treatment. He wrote at once begging her again to tell him if she were ill because his Uncle and Aunt, and even Hetty seemed to evade his questions, but when the Air Mail letter came back and assured him that she was not ill he was still not satisfied. And from the day that she left, everything at Manlands seemed to go wrong. First he was rude to his Aunt Mary and although he apologized the incident was reported to his uncle, who put him in his place in no uncertain manner. Although Charles knew that the rebuke was justified he became temperamental and made a mess of exams at school and, most foolish of all, cut two of his music lessons with Dr. Sanger in the town and went to the cinema instead. The truth is that he behaved like a stupid, spoiled small boy for the rest of the term, and was not feeling very much better when the holidays began.

This year his own school broke up on the same day as that of his cousins and by the time he got home Cyril and Derek were already there. Although his mother had begged him time and time again to do all he could to try to get on with the two boys, Charles had always found it difficult. He did not like them and was well aware that they had nothing in common. Cyril, the younger of the two, a year older than he was, wore spectacles and was much afflicted with pimples. Derek, just seventeen, was a snob of the very worst type. He was not even intelligent and never missed an opportunity of reminding Charles that a Public School education was so expensive that only the cleverest fathers could afford to send their boys to them. This summer someone had persuaded Derek that if he would do as he was told and discipline himself he might possibly be of some use at cricket as a bat.

The two boys, their mother and Charles were having tea under the big chestnut tree on the lawn on this first evening when the languid Derek looked across and said:

" Tell you what, young Charles. If you were ever lucky enough to be at our school you wouldn't be allowed to wear your hair long like that. We call it slack and sissy. Why don't you get it cut? "

" No time," Charles said through a piece of cake. " Besides I like it like this. Mother doesn't mind either."

" Nobody at our school cares what mothers like,"

Cyril explained with his usual charm, " We've just got rules—traditions we call 'em—and everybody has to keep them—or else."

" Else, then," Charles grinned. " I don't care what your traditions are. Why should I? "

" Don't answer back," Derek said. " You're the youngest here and it's time you learned to keep your place...."

" Boys! Boys! " Mrs. Strong drawled. " Do please stop this squabbling. It's much too hot. . . . Manlands has seemed so dull without my two darlings. What are you going to do to-morrow? I thought we might ask Monica and Jill over for some tennis."

Charles was used to being ignored in this way and indeed disliked these two particular girls almost as much as he hated tennis, but he was rather surprised when Derek said, " We'll see about the tennis to-morrow. Maybe we won't mind giving those girls a game some time, but I've got to practise my batting these hols. We'll put some stumps up by the tennis court and you two can bowl at me. I hope you've learned to bowl straight enough to be some use, young Charles."

This was the start of the real trouble for next afternoon Derek was foolish enough to revive the idea of cricket. Charles, who had kept out of his cousins' way most of the morning, decided that if Derek wanted batting practice he was in the mood for bowling and so he went out into the garden quite happily. It was, of course, foolish of them both to start a bitter quarrel over a game, but the trouble was that Charles, the despised younger cousin who was not even English and only went to a Grammar School, bowled much too well for the Public School boy of seventeen. Derek took the bat first, of course, and Cyril said he would bowl a few balls. The younger brother's bowling was as indifferent as Derek's batting and when the ball pitched near enough to the wicket to be hit it was hit to the elder boy's gratification. Charles did a little running about and retrieving and then, when he had realized that Derek's strokes had a certain similarity, he came in closer and caught him twice off two successive balls. This annoyed Derek who suggested a change of bowling.

Charles had the long, sensitive fingers of a musician. A master at his school, who one day had seen him playing with and twisting a tennis ball, had taken him home to tea and talked cricket to him for an hour and a half. He showed the boy what bowling could mean and something of the thrill of the battle of wits between batsman and bowler. Through most of the last summer term he had made Charles practise; taught him how to vary the flight of the ball, how to turn it and how to pitch it at exactly the right length to put his opponent in two minds. And Charles, who did not even care much for the discipline of his music master, became fascinated by the art of bowling, and although he was apt to become depressed and temperamental when he lost his length and was hit, it was not long before he was in the First Eleven and had just finished a very successful season. He found Derek easy prey and because he clean bowled him three times out of the first eight balls he forgot himself and became cocky.

" Take one of the stumps out, Derek," he suggested. " I think you're out of practice and maybe it will be fairer if I have to bowl at two instead of three."

Almost beside himself with rage Derek slashed wildly at the next ball, missed it as it broke in from leg and turned to see his off stump on the ground. There was then an awful silence which was broken by a snigger from Cyril.

Derek gulped and rather ominously suggested that Charles now take a turn with the bat.

" I'm not much good at it," the younger boy admitted, " but I'll have a go. . . . Can you bowl straight, Derek? "

Derek could not. But because of his height and his age he could fling the ball down fast and it was soon obvious that he was determined to hit Charles if he could. With a ridiculous but fanatical courage Charles, who was well aware of the other's intentions, gritted his teeth and stood firm. The fifth ball struck him a glancing blow just above the eye as he ducked to avoid it. With a roaring in his ears he dropped the bat and fell to the ground.

" You ducked," he heard Derek say. " You ran right into it. You lost your nerve and it was your own fault. You funked it."

Charles sat up and fought to keep the tears out of his eyes. He felt sick with the pain and shock and was sure that the lump above his eye was already as big as an egg. He was so angry that his voice shook.

" You did that deliberately. You're such a rotten cricketer that you can't bat and don't even know how to bowl. They wouldn't put you in our fifth eleven at school—if we had a fifth eleven. You're the sort of person who won't play any game unless you think you can win. . . ."

He got up shakily and looked up into the other's sneering face.

" You say I'm afraid. I dare you to take the bat again and although I can hardly see out of this eye I'll bowl

twelve more balls to you and I bet I'll get you out—
caught or bowled—five times. . . . Do you dare or are
you afraid? "

Derek licked his lips and glanced over his shoulder.
His mother and two girls in white shorts had just come
out on to the lawn.

" No time now," he muttered. " Got to play tennis.
You'd better cut in and put something over that eye."

" You look shocking," Cyril added. " Better not let
the girls see how your good looks have been messed
about. Try and get in the back way."

Charles dropped the bat and left them, but before
he was out of earshot he heard Derek's high-pitched
voice raised in greeting and then say—" Young Charles
has gone temperamental again. He can't play cricket and
says he won't play tennis, so I suppose he's gone
indoors. . . . No, Mother. He didn't say he was sorry.
Just saw Monica and Jill and bolted."

" Gone in to compose something wonderful I suppose," Cyril sniggered, " I'm jolly thirsty. Let's have
some cold drinks before we do anything else."

Charles slipped into the house through the scullery
door without being seen and was crossing the first landing
on the way to his room when he met his uncle, who put
a hand on his arm as he tried to hurry by.

" What have you been doing to your face, boy? "
Charles shook his head dumbly and struggled to free
himself. Mr. Strong's grip tightened.

" What have you been doing, Charles? Why aren't
you out there with the others? "

" They don't want me," Charles muttered. " You
know they don't. Nobody here wants me now my mother
has gone. . . . This bump on my eye is nothing—cricket

B

ball. . . . Let me go, please Uncle. I just want to go
to my room and be left alone. . . .

Mr. Strong had never pretended to understand his
nephew. He had tried to do his duty by him but if he
had been able to show him a little affection he would
have found that Charles might well have given him in
return more than he ever got from his own two selfish
boys. Rather dimly he mistrusted what he called Charles'
" foreign ways " and mistakenly thought that the boy
needed discipline.

" Until you learn how to behave and how to speak
to me you are better in your own room. These fits of
sulky temperament may well ruin your life one day, my
boy. . . . You must control your temper and your tongue
before mixing with decent people. . . . Go to your room
and stay there until you are ready to apologize for the
way you spoke to me just now."

Charles went thankfully enough and, as he closed the
door behind him, felt that he had reached the only haven
in a world which had nothing to offer him but bitterness,
injustice and misunderstanding. He loved this room, for
his mother, from the very earliest days at Manlands, had
taught him that it was his own and that here nobody would interfere with him. The window, with its
cushioned seat, was opposite the door and from this he
could look across the garden, through the tree tops to
the purple Shropshire hills far to the north. He had
learned to love this view as he had grown older and
watched the pageant of the changing seasons. He remembered the shape of the bare branches of the great chestnut
in winter even as he admired its opulent beauty of leaf
and blossom in the spring. He knew exactly where a

faint but brave gleam of yellow forsythia might be glimpsed from the window on Christmas Day. He knew that when the wind was in the south and brought to his open window the sound of a church clock striking four miles away that it would bring rain before morning. He had watched the rooks busy about their rebuilding operations in the elms two fields away for many springs now, and at night for the last two summers he had learned to listen for the hunting calls of the big barn owls who had now raised two families in the loft over the old stables at the back of the house.

His well-filled bookshelves were against the wall over his bed. The table for his homework was opposite. There was a cupboard with a lock and key where he kept his treasures and also a portable radio set and a very shabby, but comfortable, easy chair. It was a grand room. It was his own. His cousins never came near it and although his uncle had been there once or twice he had never brought Aunt Mary with him. Often his mother came in during the evening, and Hetty who occasionally tidied up for him was always welcome, but above all else this precious room of his was home.

He looked round quickly and then his throbbing head reminded him that he had better do something about his eye. He went across the landing to the bathroom and bathed his face in cold water and as he did so he began to shake with rage at the thought of his cousins. Why did they hate him so? He never interfered with them and what had happened to-day was entirely their own fault.

Back in his room he went to the window seat and hugging his knees looked out over the garden. He could hear the detested voices on the tennis court and the gentle and mysterious hum of a myriad insects which comes so often on a hot afternoon in high summer. The hum was soothing. He closed his eyes to ease his aching head and was soon asleep. When he woke the sun had slipped down to the west and was shining directly through the window, while the rooks cawed in the tree tops as the shadows lengthened.

He put his fingers gingerly to the lump over his eye and realized that his head was much better and then remembered what had happened a few hours ago, and that he was supposed to go to see his uncle. His resolution stiffened. He was not sure what he was going to do in the morning, but to-night he was certainly not going to apologize. Perhaps when he was really hungry he could slip out and look for Hetty who would find him some food? He listened for the voices from the garden but all was quiet now so he supposed that the girls had gone. Maybe they had all gone out in the car and left him alone, and if that were so he was happier than he had been all day.

He sat back again and began to think about his mother. Her last letter was in his pocket, and although he knew it by heart he took it out and read it through again, realizing for the twentieth time that it told him next to nothing about herself.

" . . . Stop worrying about *me,* Charles, and try and stick it out for a little longer. I know the holidays will be dull for you but do try not to squabble with your cousins. I want you to work hard at your music too—be particular about your violin practice. I was thinking about you this morning when I woke and for some odd reason caught myself remembering your tenth birthday. . . . Do you remember it . . . ? "

He put the letter back in his pocket. Yes. He remembered very well. His birthday was in March and he remembered how he had been kneeling on the window seat watching the leafless branches of the trees threshing in the gale when his mother, in her dressing-gown, had come in with the case which he knew contained his father's violin. She had kissed him, wished him many happy returns and sat down beside him, and he remembered clearly that she had talked to him that morning almost as if he were grown up, which had made him very proud.

"You are doing well with your music, Charles. Dr. Sanger is pleased with you and so am I. You know that we both want you to be a worthy son of your father and make the very best of the genius which has been passed on to you. . . . I am going to give you this—not only because I want my son to have it but because I think your father would think that his son has now earned the right to play on his violin. . . . Take it, Charles, my dear. Treasure it always and may it make music for you as it made music for your father."

With shaking fingers he opened the case and took out the lovely fiddle which he had seen many times but had never handled properly until this moment. Gently he turned it over and saw, scratched faintly upon the side, his father's signature—"Alex Renislau."

". . . . Now I have something else to tell you," his mother went on. "For almost as long as you can remember you will have heard a little tune which I have hummed or whistled to you and to myself ever since we came to England six years ago. . . ." Softly she whistled the haunting bars which, as she had said, for long had seemed almost a part of life to them both.

" I know," he had whispered. " What is it? "

" It is the theme of your father's greatest work—his Violin Concerto in C Minor. You have never heard this played for he only finished it a few months before—before we left him." She hesitated and her voice shook as she looked out over the garden that was stirring from its winter sleep, and went on, " His Concerto has never been performed in England but we believe that it has been played in Europe, although I do not know who has the original score. . . . Take the fiddle, Charles, and play your father's music for me."

Gently, with trembling fingers, he took the violin from its case again and as he played the familiar notes softly his mother turned her face away.

And from that time his father's violin became Charles' most precious possession and hardly a day passed when he did not play on it. So now, still feeling rebellious, bitter and miserable in his solitude he got off the window seat and took down the violin case from the bookshelf. In music he could usually forget everything else and so, as he had so often done before, he tuned the lovely instrument and went back to the window. The minutes slipped by and the evening shadows slid stealthily across the lawn outside as his music filled the little room and brought him peace again. Then, suddenly, with a crash, the door was slammed open and Derek with Cyril at his heels, stalked into the room. For a long minute, with bow poised, Charles stared at his cousins without speaking, feeling that something very unpleasant was going to happen, for they had never before come to his room like this. The light from the window was on their faces and he could see that although Cyril was scared the elder boy had keyed himself up for trouble. Charles, as he watched them carefully, felt again the hot uprush of rage that had so often been the cause of quarrels with them both in the past.

" Put that thing down," Derek said. " We want to talk to you and you might as well know that everybody in this house is sick of your everlasting caterwauling."

" Steady ! " Charles thought to himself. " Don't let them make you mad."

He put the violin on the table and when he spoke his voice was quite steady. " What do you want? Why can't you two leave me alone? "

" We've come to teach you manners, young Charles, because you don't seem to know how to behave when ladies are present. My mother remarked on it this afternoon when you bolted as soon as the girls arrived. . . . It's not good enough."

Charles raised his eyebrows and said nothing.

" You're always letting us down—letting the family down," Cyril put in elegantly. " That's what we want you to know. Maybe it's your school, but we're not going to have Grammar School types here."

" You talk like some brat out of a book written about fifty years ago," Charles smiled. " If you've neither of you got anything more sensible to say will you please go? "

" Oh no," Derek said as he sat on the edge of the table, " Oh no, little Charlie. You're not going to get out of this as easily as that . . . . My father told me an hour or so ago that you were sulking and that he was waiting for you to go and apologize to him. . . . We've come to fetch you to him—after we've had a little chat together."

" I don't believe you. Uncle Martin would never send you to fetch me. He's not like that."

Derek shrugged his shoulders and glanced at his brother who took up the tale.

" It's about time you did as you were told by our father. He's a very important and busy man and thousands of people have to do what they're told when he says so. Mother says it's always the same—people who owe the most to a man are always the most ungrateful and difficult. You don't seem to know what my father has done for you and your mother. It's about time that you did."

" Keep my mother out of this," Charles gasped with rising temper. " My uncle wouldn't let you talk about her like that I know, and I'll come down now and say I'm sorry if you'll come too and tell him what you've just said."

Cyril sniggered, but was careful to keep the table between him and his cousin. " That's easy to say. The sort of remark we'd expect from a Grammar School kid. . · . You tell him, Derek."

As Charles looked at the two bullies he felt a sudden little stab of apprehension. This was not because he was afraid of them physically. He knew quite well that he could deal with Cyril with one hand and probably throw him downstairs as well. Derek was not so easy for he was tall and had been full of nasty little mean tricks when they had last fought in the Christmas holidays. He was heavier now, too, but whatever the ultimate result it would be very pleasant to get in one good punch on his long nose! But in spite of this Charles was afraid because he knew them well enough to realize that they had something up their sleeves. They knew something

that he did not and were aware that they could hurt
him far more by saying something than by an honest,
straightforward fight. He had always known that they
had hated him and realized instinctively that some of this
dislike was just because he didn't do the same things!
They had often told him how they despised his music
and his school. Incidentally, Charles had met enough
Public School boys to know that they were not like his
cousins and that half the troubles of Derek and Cyril
were due to the fact that they were very unpopular at
their own school and would be wherever they went.
He was neither old enough nor shrewd enough to understand that these two spoiled and unhappy boys were
jealous of his natural good manners and ability, but he
was just beginning to realize that nothing had made
Derek more bitter and angry than his failure with a
cricket bat. This flashed through his mind as he stood
there in the dusk with his back to the window, fearing
that he was to be hurt by something they were going
to tell him. Perhaps it was something to do with his
mother? They knew quite well that it was through her
that he could be most hurt. Perhaps they were going
to tell him the real truth about her going away? Perhaps
—the old fear came rushing back—perhaps she was
seriously ill and they were keeping the news from him,
although it never occurred to him as odd that Derek
and Cyril should know about such an illness while he
was in ignorance.

He sighed and his voice shook a little as he stepped
forward and said, " Speak up then if you've got something to say. I can't stop you talking. I only wish I
could. I hate the sight of you both, even more than I
hate the sound of your voices."

Of course they had worked it all out between them in advance. They knew exactly what they were going to say and it didn't really take very long. Derek did most of the talking and his thin, sneering, supercilious voice pattered on through the dusk until Charles almost wondered if he were dreaming.

" You're old enough to know that you only live at Manlands because of my father's kindness. You're dependent on him as you have been ever since you came here before the war. . . . You don't seem to realize how lucky you are to be living in a place like this and meeting the sort of people we meet. . . ."

Dimly Charles heard a voice which he did not recognize as his own.

" . . . Are you saying all this about my Mother too? Do you dare say that? "

Derek shifted uneasily.

" Of course I don't pretend to know what sort of arrangement your mother has with my father, but it's obvious to everyone that you can't really afford to live here. Surely you can see that? Surely that's plain even to you? "

Charles felt his knees weaken under him and sat down.

" You can't know what you're saying, Derek. What do you mean? Why are you telling these lies? " he gasped.

Just for a moment the elder boy hesitated and it seemed that he might, after all, be ashamed of what he was saying. Then Cyril spoke up from the other side of the table.

" You're dumb, aren't you? Have we got to tell you straight out that you're not wanted here? Think that over," and he turned to go out of the door.

*He managed to get the violin on to the window seat
behind him. . . .*

Charles jumped to his feet.

"You miserably, pimply little rat!" he shouted.
"Just let me get hold of you and I can soon make you
understand what I think of you," and he sprang forward.

Derek pushed him back and made a grab for the
violin.

"And we're sick and tired of this everlasting
squeaking and wailing which you call music," he began,
but got no further, for Charles, prepared to put up with
a great deal, would never allow either of these two to
touch his fiddle. He never really knew what happened
during the next few minutes except that he managed
to get the violin on to the window seat behind him and
then turned to fight the two of them. And he must have

fought like a fury for somehow he drove them from the room, although Cyril did not stay for long.

Vaguely he was aware of Derek's scared face as he flew at him with everything he knew about boxing forgotten. Twice the elder boy flung him to the floor but each time he was up as quickly as he was down and although his own nose was bleeding Derek's face soon showed the scars of battle.

Then, quite suddenly, he was alone. The door slammed behind his tormentors. Gasping, sobbing with rage and with blood trickling down his face he turned the key in the lock and went back to the window seat. The evening outside was still as lovely and peaceful. The rooks were still circling and cawing above the distant elms and the shadows were just a little longer. Everything in the outside world was the same, but inside the little room which for so long had been his citadel, Charles' own particular world crumbled into ruins. Black eyes and broken noses mattered little in comparison with the disillusionment he now felt. Even though his cousins may well have made up the whole story there was enough poison in it to make him wonder if he was really unwanted. He had always known that his Aunt Mary disliked him but never had his austere uncle ever suggested in any way that he was unwanted here. True, he had never shown him much affection, but Charles could not believe that for all these years he had really been unwelcome. The taunt that hurt most was that he was really living at Manlands on charity, but he knew that they would never have dared to say this if his mother had been at home.

Slowly, as it grew darker, and a few bats fluttered crazily outside the window, Charles saw that he must run away and prove, at least until his mother returned, that he could support himself.

The more he considered this idea the more attractive it became. To run off and leave the lot of them. He'd go in the night, with a knapsack and his fiddle. Surely he could earn his keep by playing his fiddle? Why not? Perhaps he could join a fair or a circus, but wherever he went he would make music. Sleep under haystacks, of course. But would it be better to take his bike or hitch hike? That was one thing to be decided and the other was when and how he was going to apologize to his uncle, and as he thought this over he realized that he must write to him and say he was sorry and tell him something of what he intended to do. Better to be honest about it.

He crossed the room and took up his pen and a sheet of paper.

CHAPTER TWO

THE ROAD TO ADVENTURE

CHARLES sat for a long time at his table with a sheet of paper before him and a pen in his hand. The twilight of the summer evening faded into dusk until it was too dark for him to see to write. After a little he began to wonder why nobody else had been up to see him for the house was strangely quiet. He was hungry, too, and his head ached and he could feel that his lips were broken and swollen.

It was after ten o'clock and he had not even switched on the light when there came a knock on the door and a well-known voice said quietly:

" Are you asleep, Master Charles? "

" No, Hetty. I wish I was."

She tried the door. " Let me in, boy, and tell me your troubles."

" No, Hetty. It's decent of you but I don't want to talk to-night. I'm all right but I want to be left alone."

" Don't be silly, Charles. You've been up here for hours and you've been in trouble, too, and what's more you've had nothing to eat. . . . Will I be bringing you up a little something on a tray? "

He got up, unlocked the door and held it open a few inches.

" You're grand, Hetty," he said, " but I don't want anything to-night and I don't feel like talking to you. . . . I'm going to bed in a sec. . . . I was just sitting and thinking."

"It's not sitting and thinking you ought to be doing, boy, but eating and then sleeping. . . . Switch on that light and let me have a look at you. I can see your face is swollen. Have you been fighting with those two again?"

Charles grinned and then winced with pain.

"I have, and you should see their faces—specially dear Cyril's. . . . Good night, Hetty See you in the morning," and he gently closed the door, switched on the light and went back to the table. He knew now quite definitely what he was going to do and characteristically, once he had made up his mind, he wasted no more time.

The letter which he wrote to his uncle took him nearly two hours to finish. Some of it, of course, was very schoolboyish, and some of it was rather silly, but it was all very sincere. If we were looking over his shoulder as the words flowed from his pen these are some of the paragraphs which we should have been able to read.

Dear Uncle Martin,

First of all I want to say I am sorry if I was rude to you this afternoon. I didn't mean to be rude or sulky but I was fed up after a row with Derek and Cyril just because I kept bowling out Derek, who isn't much good at cricket anyway, and I wasn't feeling too good about it. . . .

I am very unhappy and fed up ever since Mother went away and this isn't just because she isn't here nor because I'm worried about whether she's ill, but because I'm beginning to feel that none of you want me but just put up with Mother and me because you're really kind. . . .

I think I ought to tell you that I had an awful fight

*with Cyril and Derek this evening. I tried not to do this
and even after they'd told me that none of you really
wanted me I tried not to scrap but I couldn't help it
when they began to fool about with my Father's fiddle.
You know what I think about Father, don't you, sir?
Nothing anybody says could make me change my mind
about my Father and when Derek grabbed for the fiddle
and ragged me about my music I lost my temper and
we all bashed each other about and I know you'll be
mad with us but that's how it happened and I'm afraid
I'm not really sorry about the scrap. . . .*

*But what I really want to say now, sir, is that I have
decided not to be a burden to you any longer. I don't
mean to be rude but I know Aunt Mary doesn't like
me and the others told me to-day that I'm not wanted
here. I don't want to be where I'm not wanted, so until
my Mother comes back or lets me know what she's going
to do I am going away. Please don't send anybody after
me, Uncle. I have got a little money and I have taken
some food from the pantry which I will pay back one
day. I am not going to do anything silly but I want
to show you that I can keep myself and look after myself
without anybody's help. I know now that I'm not wanted
here but I shall write to explain to Mother when she is
better and perhaps I can make enough money by playing
the fiddle to take her away and keep her too. Anyway
I'm going to try, and please don't write to Mother and
worry her just because I've done this. I'll write to her
myself when I think I should and explain. . . .*

*Please let me alone and don't interfere. I shall be all
right but I'm not coming back until I've proved that
I can keep myself and earn my own living without
bothering anybody. Of course it will be much more diffi-*

cult for me to keep Mother when she comes back, but I expect she'll come with me when she understands why I've done this. She always understands. She's wonderful and I wish I knew why she's gone away. Maybe I can get over there to see her when I've made enough money. . . .

I suppose I ought to say " Thank you very much " for keeping me at Manlands for such a long time. I have always been very keen on this room you let me have but as I don't really know how you arranged everything with Mother about all the food we eat I can't do any more about it except to say " Thank you " again for that. . . . I'm sorry that I can't get on with Cyril and Derek but I can't. Mother often told me I must. I'm sorry too if you think I'm sulky but I'm not feeling sulky now. I feel excited. . . .

There is just one more thing. I know you think I'm crazy about my music and not like ordinary boys. Well, my Father was a very great musician and I'm going to be one too one day. Not as good as him, of course, because it may be a hundred years before there's anyone else as good, but I'm going to try. After Mother, music is the most important and wonderful thing to me and although I'm not saying this very well now because I'm tired and it's late and I've been writing for a long time, I want everybody to understand this. . . .

Sorry, but there's one more thing. Besides the food I've borrowed from the kitchen I may have to borrow one of your maps from your study. I won't disturb anything else and I'll send it back when I've used it.

Lots of times you have been jolly decent to me, Uncle, and thank you very much for them.

Charles.

c

PS. Cyril and Derek will be pleased I've gone because that's what they wanted. They'll be able to have some wonderful cricket practice too, because they'll never get each other out.

As he wrote the last word he tried to smile through his broken lips and then sat back and yawned. His watch said ten to twelve. He went to the window and leaned over the sill. The night was dark blue and silver and very still. The moon was up and the shadows of the trees across the lawn were as sharp and clear as if they had been cut from black paper and laid flat on velvet, and Charles thought that the roses had never smelled more exquisitely. Nor had he ever realized before just how important and wonderful the sense of smell can be. The peace of the night and this new experience of beauty began to form tentative little tunes in his head. He began to translate them into music and then, as the barn owl sailed silently across the lawn, the spell was broken, and the only music in his mind was the old familiar theme of the Renislau Concerto.

He sighed and turned away from the window. Without reading through the long letter to his uncle—it would have been very unlike Charles to have done such a thing —he shuffled the sheets together and stuffed them into an envelope which he sealed. Then, very quietly, he went to his clothes cupboard and brought out the rucksack his mother gave him two years ago. Next he changed. Corduroy trousers, grey shirt and lumber jacket. Into the knapsack he stuffed a spare shirt and a dark blue pullover with a high collar, but this didn't seem very much on which to start an adventure so he found two pairs of socks and a tie and put them in too. Then he opened the door, crept out on to the landing and crossed to the bathroom for toothbrush, soap and sponge. It took him a long time to find a rubber bag to put them in and it was ten minutes past midnight when he left his room. He hated doing this. Everything that had happened in his life since he had come to England was somehow crystallized inside these four walls. This room was far more real to him than school; meant far more than Dr. Sanger's studio with its pale green walls. Here were all his treasures—Christmas and birthday presents, his beloved books, piles of untidy music, the radio, and gramophone records of his own which he used on his uncle's radiogram downstairs. On the top of the cupboard beside the tennis racquet, which was about the only thing he would not miss, he noticed, as he took a last look round, the old cigar box with eight bird's eggs in it. He had soon tired of collecting eggs but suddenly these trophies of a short-lived craze three springs ago seemed very important.

It was no use waiting, anyway, so he slung the knapsack on his back, picked up his stoutest shoes and the violin case, switched out the light and crept out on to the landing with an unpleasant, tight feeling in his throat. The moonlight streamed through the window at the turn of the staircase so that it was easy for him to pick his way down, but he stopped twice in a panic as the stairs creaked under his stockinged feet. It was on the next landing that the family slept and when he reached it his heart was thudding painfully with excitement. But the carpet was soft and his feet made no sound, and in another minute he was in the hall. He stood very still and listened as the grandfather clock in the corner ticked solemnly, and then moved forward. His uncle's study was the second room on the left and as he wanted the most unpleasant job over first he turned the door handle firmly and walked in very much more boldly than he felt. He had never liked this room, possibly because its main associations were connected with unpleasant interviews. It looked just as forbidding and austere in moonlight and he was almost surprised not to see the stern figure of his uncle sitting behind the desk. Mr. Strong was a tidy man and Charles was quite sure that having once decided that the left-hand end of second shelf up in the alcove to the right of the window was the best place to keep maps, nothing thereafter would alter this decision. He was quite right. There they were —a neat pile of folding maps so that it was possible to get at them with the minimum discomfort. He switched on the hooded light on the desk, took down the maps and began to go through them. He was not at all sure where he was going except that eventually it ought to be Switzerland, but he chose a map of their own district first, and then two more which covered territory to the south. He stuffed them into the pocket of his haversack and was about to switch out the light when he noticed a pencil with a new point in the pentray. The blotting-paper on the desk pad was clean, of course, and he was a little apprehensive as he wrote on it, " *I have borrowed three maps. Thank you very much. C."*

Everything was quiet again in the hall but he felt a sense of relief when he closed the green baize service door behind him and found himself in the kitchen. He switched on the light, put his shoes, knapsack and violin on the table and went through to explore the pantry. Now that he was faced with a decision it was rather difficult to know what to take. There were two bottles of milk in the refrigerator and the remains of two cold

THE ROAD TO ADVENTURE

chickens, and the sight of these reminded him that he had had nothing to eat since lunch. Perhaps it would be wiser to have a picnic now and then just take a few sandwiches with him in case of emergency? He sat down at the kitchen table and drank nearly a pint of milk from the bottle and then started on the chicken and some bread. He sat with his back to the door and was just tearing at a leg bone when he had the horrible feeling that he was being watched. With his hair tickling on his scalp he took the bone from his lips and turned his head very slowly—slowly because he was afraid of what he would see.

In the doorway stood a little old lady wearing a scarlet, wool dressing-gown. She stood with one hand on the half-open door while the other fidgeted with her spectacles. Her hair was grey and wispy and her feet, nearly covered by the length of her white nightdress, were in old bedroom slippers. As Charles stared at her open-mouthed, she closed the door very gently behind her, took a step towards him, and smiled.

" So there you are, boy. I thought I heard you go down and followed you as soon as I could. . . . I would have brought you up something to eat, Master Charles. No need to go creeping about the house like a horrid burglar."

Charles smiled in relief and welcome.

" Hetty! I can't stand another shock like that. Why didn't you knock? Come in and have a bite of chicken, although I haven't left much."

Her glance moved to the knapsack on the table and a flicker of apprehension showed in her eyes.

" What are you dressed up like this for? Where are you going? "

"I don't know, Hetty. Just out into the cold, hard world to seek my fortune."

"You're daft, boy! Stay where you are and I'll be making us a cup of tea, and then you can tell me all about it."

He munched a piece of cake and watched her affectionately. He was very fond of Hetty and was feeling much better than when he had last argued with her through the half-open door of his room, but it was not going to be easy to tell her the truth.

Not until the tea was poured out did she speak again. Then, as she handed him his cup, "I knew right well that you were up to something. I was awake and listening for you, for 'twasn't natural for you to go so long without food unless you were ill and that you were not. . . . And I knew you'd been fighting again of course, because"—a grim little smile hovered round her lips— "I've seen them other two, but fun's fun and now you can just tell me what you're up to."

"I'm clearing out," he said and with a sudden flush of shame realized that he had intended to go without seeing Hetty or leaving a note for her. "I'm fed up with those two in particular and I'm fed up without Mother and not knowing what's the matter with her and why she doesn't come back. . . . You know what it is. Sometimes," he added shrewdly, "I think you know better than Mother just how rotten it is for me here."

She nodded. "Maybe I know all sorts of things. But what's happened special to-day? It's not the first time you've had a fight with those two, is it? What's made you decide to run away?"

He looked up sharply at the last two words. "I didn't say I was running away."

" But you are. That's just what you are doing. You don't like it and you're running away."

Charles lifted his hand and pushed back the lock of hair from his forehead. " And what's more," Hetty said remorselessly as she curled her old fingers round her cup, " you're running away when your mother's not here. For all you know she may want you to stick it out at Manlands."

" I don't think she would," Charles replied soberly. " Honestly I don't, Hetty. . . . Derek told me to-night that Mother and I are both living here on Uncle's—charity. . . . He told me, too, that I'm not wanted at Manlands and never have been, so I'm going away for a bit to think it over. . . . Would you like me to tell you any more? "

She was looking down at her cup now and her cheeks were flushed as she whispered, " Did he really say that to you? " and then, unexpectedly, and almost under her breath, " The little rat."

But Charles heard her and knew on that instant that he had found an ally. He got up, went round to her, sat on the edge of the table and put an arm round her thin shoulders. He knew how to get his own way with her.

" That's what I think of him too, Hetty, and you'll help me, won't you? I've written a long letter to Uncle Martin and I'm going to leave it on the hall table for him. I've told him that I'm going off on my own just to prove that if I'm not wanted here I can jolly well be independent."

" But how can you, boy? Have you got any money? "

" About thirty bob, but I'm going to earn my way. I reckon I can earn my food, Hetty, by doing odd jobs

and playing the fiddle. The weather is good, I'm going
on my bike, I'll take a mack and I can sleep out. It'll
be fun. I feel happier than at any time since Mother
went away. . . . You'll help me won't you, Hetty?
You won't stop me going now? I mean you won't go
and wake them up and tell them you've caught me
raiding the pantry? "

For a moment she laid her hand on his in an
odd caress and when she looked up at him there were
tears in her eyes.

" You're crazy, boy. You're as wilful and headstrong
as your mother, but I'll help you—or I won't stop you
—on one condition."

" Before you tell me that, tell me the truth about
Mother. Why has she gone to Switzerland and when
will she be back? "

She refused to meet his eyes.

" I don't know the truth, Charles, but I promise you
faithfully that I don't think she's ill. She told you, and
she told me, not to worry and that she'd be back when
she could. From the moment she was born I've loved
her and trusted her and I still do. . . . But I wish I
knew all the same," she whispered almost to herself.

" Very well," he said as his voice hardened, " But
it's not fair of her. . . . What's your one condition,
Hetty? "

" Only that you'll ring up if you're in real trouble
and that you'll keep in touch with me somehow. . . .
Your uncle is all right underneath, Master Charles, and
you do wrong to annoy and upset him. . . . I say nothing
about those other two and if you want to go out camping
on your own this weather I don't see why you shouldn't
—specially as your mother isn't here. . . . But promise

me you'll keep in touch, boy, for I must know where you are. A message might come from your mother any day."

" So it might, Hetty. Suppose there's a letter for me in the morning? What should we do? How shall I know? Uncle wouldn't open it if it was addressed to me, would he? "

She got up from the table and shook her head.

" I don't know, but I reckon he wouldn't. . . . There's only one thing for it, Master Charles—I'll have to keep an eye on the letter box and then act as postman for you."

" Do you really mean you'll keep a lookout and hide any letter for me? You're a darling, Hetty. Really you are. I promise I'll let you know where I am every now and then and I promise if anything goes wrong that I'll ring up. But I won't let any of them know if I'm beaten and I won't come back unless I have to. What I'd like to do is to stay away all the holidays or until Mother comes back. . . . I've not had time to think what I'll do after the hols. yet."

" It will be raining by then," Hetty replied drily, " and you'll be pleased of a roof over your head even if it's only this one, but I don't altogether blame you for going off now. . . . What have you got in that haversack thing? "

He held it out apprehensively.

" Travelling light, aren't you? Better get your thin mack and I'll pack it in properly for you, then we'll see about some more food."

All was quiet in the house when he went out again into the hall. The grandfather clock ticked on remorselessly and the moonlight spilled in a pool across the floor.

When he got back Hetty had been to the pantry.

" I don't know what's come over me I'm sure," she muttered. " I reckon I'll have to tell cook I was taken queer in the night and had to get myself something to eat."

" You needn't worry, Hetty. As soon as Uncle reads my letter they'll know I've done it. If you're afraid of being blamed for something you didn't do I'll leave another message and explain. I've written a note on his blotting pad and I've said in the long letter that I'm taking some food, so nobody will think you've been raiding the pantry for yourself."

" Aiding and abetting—that's what it is," she murmured as she cut off some slices of corned beef. " I don't know what's come over me."

Charles laughed. He was beginning to feel excited again. " I only hope that's dear Cyril's meat ration, but I bet he wouldn't go without. He'd take Aunt Mary's share."

She smiled grimly as she crammed the last sandwich into a paper bag and pushed the latter into the haversack.

" There you are! Not very elegant but you won't starve for a few hours. There's cake in there too and some biscuits. And if you're going now you'd better be off."

" But Hetty! " he was obviously worried about this. " What are you going to say or do in the morning when they find I've gone? How are you going to be surprised? Or aren't you? "

" You leave that to me, boy. I'll do my best to keep any letters from your mother that come for you but it won't be easy, and you'll promise to write me or telephone and let me know how everything goes and if you want any help—and when you're coming back," she added with a smile.

As he stooped to tie his shoe laces he suddenly felt miserable. " And when you're coming back," made him remember that in spite of everything this was his only home, and that even if he didn't like Derek and Cyril and Aunt Mary there was his mother, and Hetty, and every now and then his uncle, and the chaps at school and his music—though he knew he'd have that somehow or other wherever he went—and his room and the rooks in the tree tops over the garden, and white candles of blossom on the chestnut tree in the spring.

" I'll come back, Hetty," he said as he straightened his back. " Of course I shall. But I'm going to have some fun just to prove I can do something without anybody's help."

She was too wise to remind him that it isn't really possible for anybody to do anything without somebody's help and so she just smiled at him as he went to the back door.

" Thanks about keeping the letters, Hetty. I won't worry if I know you've got them safe. When I ring up maybe you could read them over to me. . . . I say, Hetty. I've just thought of something. The telephone will be difficult. P'raps they won't let me talk to you. Maybe they'll say you're out and maybe you will be. . . . I'll have to disguise my voice, Hetty. I'll have to pretend to be your boy friend! "

" Get along with you do," she laughed. " I'll look after myself and tell them what I think I should. If you ask for me on the telephone I shall be fetched, but you can write every day if you like and let me know that all is well. . . . Have you got everything? "

*" If you've made up your mind to go you'd better
go now."*

He leaned forward in the dark and kissed her
awkwardly on her wrinkled cheek.

" Don't worry, Hetty. I'll manage somehow and I
promise I'll come back."

" I've no doubt of that, my boy. What will you do
if your uncle tells the police? They'll catch you easily
enough and you'll be brought back here with your tail
between your legs."

" You don't really think he'd do that? " He hadn't
thought of the police. " I've told him in the letter that
I'm going to prove I can keep myself. There's nothing
wrong in that is there? Besides if I'm not wanted here
they won't send the police after me."

She put her hands on his shoulders.

" I'll back you up, boy but if you've made up your mind to go you'd better go now. Good luck! What have you done with the letter to Mr. Strong? "

" I'm not much good at this really, Hetty," he admitted ruefully, " It's still in my pocket. Will you put it on the hall table for me, please? "

He passed it over without noticing the tender little smile about her lips, but before he could say more she pushed him gently over the step and closed the door in his astonished face. The lock clicked home and in a sudden moment of panic he realized that he had burned his boats. Perhaps Hetty had an idea that it might be good for him if he did? She had known him intimately for nearly ten years and sometimes saw him more clearly even than did his mother.

Charles hitched the knapsack on to his back, picked up the violin case and, treading carefully on the grass verge so that his shoes on the gravel would not betray him, walked in the moonlight down to the shed where the bicycles were kept.

The latch clicked loudly as he lifted it but there was enough light for him to wheel the cycle into the open without making any noise. He checked the tyres and even remembered to make sure that he had tools and a puncture outfit and that both lamps worked. At the last minute he realized that his pump was missing and was not altogether surprised when he found it on Cyril's bicycle. Next he took his mackintosh from the knapsack and packed it into the saddle bag and then, after strapping the violin case to the carrier, he closed the door of the shed and cycled down the drive to the front gate. The moonlight was so bright that he could see the individual roses on the bushes bordering the lawn—

roses which might well have been touched by Midas so cold, colourless and metallic did they appear. The gravel popped and slithered under the impact of his hard tyres and almost before he realized it he was through the open gate of Manlands and in the shadow of the lane.

Until now he had been too excited to consider where he was going, but as he cycled through the lovely, sweet-smelling summer night he realized that if he was to make a real success of this venture he must soon make a plan. There was not much he did not know about the ten miles of country round Manlands and he realized that even in the middle of the night it would be as well to avoid towns and main roads. After ten minutes' riding he stopped at a familiar cross roads and sat down in the bracken at the foot of a signpost to consider the position. He realized that if he wanted to pay his way by doing odd jobs and playing the fiddle he would have to go where there were people, and that meant towns. If by any chance his uncle did inform the police he supposed that they would take the same view and look for him in such places. They might, of course, think that he would make for London eventually, so, to begin with, it would probably be advisable for him to go in the opposite direction. This meant riding north, and the north meant Ludlow and the Shropshire hills, and the little towns and villages in wild country where surely he could begin to make a living. And there was the advantage too that he would not be too far from Manlands if he had to go back for a letter.

Besides, there was something about Ludlow that thrilled him although he had not been there many times, and as he sat in the moonlight at the foot of the sign-post he remembered again the broad street leading up to the narrow arch on the way to the ruins of the mighty castle at the top of the hill. He remembered the great tower of the church of St. Lawrence and the beautiful river which runs round the hill on which the town is built, and swirls under the old stone bridge which is too narrow for traffic to pass upon it. He remembered with pleasure, too, one of the most attractive ironmonger's shops he had ever seen and an equally interesting café almost opposite. He remembered the many legends and stories he had read about Ludlow and the Welsh Marches and thought " That's the place for me. It may be a town but I don't believe they'll think I've gone that way. Maybe I'll get as far to-night! "

But he didn't. It may have been because he was so tired, or possibly because he could not always read the signposts when they were in shadow, but he soon lost his way. At first he merely said to himself, " Funny, I don't remember this bit," and cycled on in the hope that he would soon recognize a landmark. Soon after he realized that none of the pointing fingers of the signposts now mentioned Ludlow. Common sense advised that he should go back until he found a directed crossroads, but he was getting very tired and sleepy and had not the heart to do so. Surely this road, which was little better than a lane, must lead somewhere? He was as certain as he could be that he was riding towards the north, but he was puzzled to know where he had missed the way.

At two o'clock he was pushing his cycle up a hill arched with trees and decided that he could go no farther until he had eaten, rested and slept.

At the top of the hill the country spread out and with the trees left behind he realized that he was on the edge of wide, wild and open common or heath. For a mile or more ahead of him the road wound like a twisted ribbon between the gorse and heather, but he could go no farther. A few yards from the road to his left was a little pit in the sand, rather like the bunker on a golf course. It was edged with heather and a bush of broom shielded it on one side, and to Charles it looked inviting.

He pushed his bicycle off the road and then dropped it thankfully at the edge of the pit. Next he unpacked his mackintosh and spread it out over the soft sand and put on his blue pullover. His knapsack made a hard pillow but it was tolerably comfortable when he curled himself under the bank. He was asleep in a few minutes.

CHAPTER 3

THE BUCKINGHAMS

THE common on which Charles slept on the first night of his adventure is not many miles from Ludlow and is known as Leasend. It is a wild and lonely heath seeming rather out of place on the edge of hill country and, at the northern end, where it narrows, stands an old house of the same name.

Some say that once this house was an inn, although it cannot have enjoyed much custom in so lonely a position, but it is almost certain that it was once used as a farmhouse; yet, as its present owner, Mr. Buckingham, sometimes remarked, the only animals which would have survived on the poor pasture round about would have been goats or mules.

Mr. Buckingham is an author who prefers to work in the peace of the country. On the day when he first passed Leasend in a car twelve years ago he decided that this was where he was going to live eventually and where he would write his greatest book! It was lucky for him that his wife shared his enthusiasm for it was asking rather a lot of a mother with two babies to move into a new home where the domestic conveniences were so few. But the charm of Leasend touched her too, and when they moved in Juliet was three and a half and her brother, Simon, two.

Some families fit some houses at once and Mr. Buckingham's instinct about Leasend was right, for life there had run as smoothly as any family had a right to expect. Mr. Buckingham had converted an old granary into a study where he could work undisturbed by the clamour of his growing family, and even if he had not yet produced his greatest book he did, at least, keep on trying! His wife, with a strange assortment of helpers over the years, managed to turn the accommodating house into a real home, tended the garden with loving care, raised flowers, fruit, vegetables, poultry and bees, and steered Juliet and Simon safely into adolescence. Her children were by far the most complicated and exciting of her problems.

It was natural enough that they should both grow up with a real love of the countryside and from their earliest days at Leasend they learned instinctively about birds, flowers and trees and how to care for animals. They learned not to fuss about the weather, too, and how to make the best of summer and winter, for as soon as they were old enough and conditions made it possible, they cycled daily to Ludlow to school, although at the time we first meet them Simon has just come from his first term at a Public School.

Although they both made friends easily—Juliet even more quickly than her brother—their strongest attachment was to their parents and their home. The Buckinghams were not only a loyal and united family but one in which parents and children shared a very rare companionship. There were no jealousies between brother and sister and there was real friendship between the four of them. It was natural enough that this should be a cultured home if it was not a wealthy one, and the children were often secretly amazed that so many other of the homes into which they went should have so few books, papers, pictures and music. Simon and his mother were fairly methodical and tidy, while father and daughter were the very opposite.

Juliet, who almost from the time she could speak had made up her mind to be an actress, was really beautiful. Her hair, which she wears to her shoulders and parts almost over her left ear, is nearly fair enough to be ash blonde. She is slightly built but carries herself more like a woman than a schoolgirl and is already an inch taller than her tiny mother. Her secret prayers are that she will grow at least another three inches for it is difficult to be an actress of outstanding ability if you are short! Her eyes are a deep blue and wide enough to suggest a deceptive air of incredulity and innocence. The greatest mistake which a stranger can make is to treat Juliet Buckingham as a child, for although not particularly clever nor practical she is extremely intelligent with a great sense of fun and adventure, and the poise and natural good manners which come only from the background of a good home.

Simon is rather more like his amusing father, with the same nondescript good looks. He has more brains than Juliet and is certainly quicker witted but inclined to be indolent. Boarding school is going to be very good for him, but although at home he is a little overshadowed by his striking and impulsive sister, he will almost certainly do something really worth-while one day.

While Charles Renislau was still sleeping in a sand-pit a mile and a half away at the other end of Leasend Common Juliet was waking to greet another exciting day. There was no particular reason why she should wake so early except that the sun was streaming across the end of her bed through the open window. She sat up, stretched luxuriously and sniffed. It was a grand

morning. She clasped her knees and leaned forward to
see the ripening fruit already bending the boughs of the
old apple tree outside her window. There is only one
country smell more satisfying than the scent of rain
on dry soil and that is the rich enticement of a well-
stocked garden early on a sunny summer morning when
the air is still fresh and clean. July is not the month of
bird song and it was very quiet and still as she lay back
on her pillow and gazed up at the ceiling. Her lips
moved almost as if she were saying her prayers and then,
because she was alone and Simon was not there to tease
her, she said softly:

> " Shall I compare thee to a summer's day?
> Thou art more lovely and more temperate;
> Rough winds do shake the darling buds of May,
> And summer's lease hath all too short a date."

She repeated the last line almost greedily and then sighed,
" Lovely! Lovely! P'raps I woke early just to remember
that? One day perhaps I'll be able to stand up in front
of hundreds of people with the lights on me and say
that sonnet to the end and make them all FEEL that
someone once said to me ' But thy eternal summer shall
not fade ' on a heavenly morning like this. . . . Oh!
What a fool I am! " and she blushed violently, jumped
out of her bed and ran to the window.

The morning was as lovely as it smelled. Her room
was at the side of the house overlooking part of the
lawn and flower garden and an old flint wall with its
coping of warm brick which just here ran alongside
the road. There was still a suspicion of mist over the
common and she knew that it was going to be very hot
later—the sort of day when school would have been

unreasonable but one that was ideal for the holidays. A Red Admiral butterfly, encouraged by the early sunshine, floated by just below her and she almost cried out with excitement as she recognized a goldfinch busy among the seed heads of a thistle against the wall. On the far side of the road on the common was a patch of soft gold which she knew to be lady's bedstraw because it had appeared every year in this same place for as long as she could remember.

"This is going to be a lovely day to do things in," she thought. "Maybe we ought to go to Ludlow and swim, but bikes will be rather a fag. I wonder if the parents have any plans? Maybe Daddy could be persuaded not to work and would take us somewhere in the vehicle."

While she was still pondering over this she had what she described as one of her beautiful thoughts. "I'll go and make some tea and bring it up to them all and then I'll get breakfast in the garden."

She washed and dressed herself in a yellow shirt and blue shorts and went downstairs feeling a trifle smug. She put on the kettle, tickled the cat and put four cups on a tray. While waiting for the water to boil she wandered into the lounge and opened the windows while the cat followed her purring and pushing against her legs.

She glanced at the clock and saw that it was not yet seven o'clock and then turned over the pile of gramophone records on a chair. A little music to fit the morning seemed indicated but it was not a very easy choice. A symphony would be too solemn and too long, and the Greig *Piano Concerto* had been heard too many times. She paused before rejecting Yehudi Menuhin playing

Bach's *Violin Concerto in E Major* and then pounced happily on the ballet music from *Swan Lake*. The Buckinghams did not often go to London and so did not see much ballet, but Juliet had enjoyed *Swan Lake* twice and could see again almost every movement of the enchanting dance by the four little black swans as the music changed to the loved and familiar tune that heralded their entrance. When the Cygnets' dance was over she started the record again and found the kettle boiling over when she got back to the kitchen.

Ten minutes later she was sitting on the end of her father's bed while a disgruntled and tousled Simon was honouring his mother in the same way.

" I don't care what she says or what sort of a beautiful morning it is," he was saying as he waved a half-empty tea cup in emphasis, " I just don't think it's natural to wake a chap up at seven o'clock so early in the hols. and then ask him to drink tea."

" You're a slug," Juliet replied. " A lazy little slug. Little boys are horrible in the morning. They don't wake up full of the joy of life, all alert and intelligent like— like I do," she finished modestly.

" Neither do some big boys," her father groaned. " Get off my feet, darling. . . . I'm nearly always pleased to see you, Juliet, and we appreciate your lovely thought this morning, but you are sometimes a little *sudden*. . . . Your entry into this room with that tray just now, for instance, was a trifle precipitate. I'm getting on in years now and— " but the rest of the sentence was lost in the hoots and jeers of his children. Juliet got off his bed and looked down at him affectionately. He *was* a nice father. Small and crinkly and brown, rather like Puck in *Puck of Pook's Hill* as she had once told him.

" Go away now, children," Mrs. Buckingham said sleepily from the other bed, " and thank you very much for the tea, Juliet. . . . And if you're going to get the breakfast in the garden—and it's a lovely idea—do try and do it efficiently."

When they were outside the bedroom door Simon grinned maliciously. " Now I'm going back to bed. You're so full of beautiful, unselfish thoughts this morning that I'd hate to interfere with them. I hope they last all day."

He dodged into the bathroom as she grabbed at him and then put his head round the door. " I say, Julie . . . I'm serious about this. Have the parents said anything about real summer holidays? I mean are we going away somewhere? We ought to. Everybody else does. Now I'm away at school nobody tells me anything."

His sister shook her head.

" I don't know, Simon. They haven't said anything but Daddy is halfway through his new book and rather temperamental and touchy, and you know what *that* means. I think he'll finish it before we do go away, but I haven't asked. Buck up and come down and give me a hand."

" I shall ask him," Simon said. " We've got to know. I shall be very polite about it, but of course I shall be firm."

He was down in ten minutes and together they dragged the old garden table out of the loggia into the shade of the chestnut tree. The mist was disappearing now and in the long bed under the flint wall the bees were already busy about the closed mouths of the gay, coloured snapdragons, while a little haze of heat shimmered over the road which stretched like a strip of white ribbon over the common into the distance.

When Mr. and Mrs. Buckingham came down the table was laid, the coffee made and four boiled eggs were ready under the little covers which Juliet with willing, but inexperienced fingers, had knitted for the family many years ago.

Then the postman's van drew up and Simon went over to the gate to greet him.

" Yes thanks," the others heard him say, " It's nice to be back for the hols. I've had a terrible time really but I don't complain. They all thought it was best for me to go away to school and they don't seem to care what I go through. . . . Try and bring me lots of letters now that I'm back. . . . Cheerio."

Mr. Buckingham sat down with the air of business-like precision with which he tried to begin each day and took the pile of mail which Simon passed him a little apprehensively. Simon always felt a trifle nervous until the ordeal of his report was over and somehow he felt that this new one would lead to some worrying questions. While his father sorted his correspondence into what he called the " the sheep and the goats," which meant that all unsealed envelopes bearing penny stamps and likely to contain bills were left unopened until he was in the mood to consider them. Mrs. Buckingham glanced warningly at Juliet while this sorting was in progress for she knew, from long experience, how a chance remark at this time could ruin a breakfast. When the sorting was complete and Simon was sure that the only long, narrow envelope contained nothing harmful, he relaxed and upset the carton of cornflakes.

" Ha! " said Mr. Buckingham as he tore up a letter and reached for the toast and, " Thanks," as he took his coffee and, "Nonsense! I won't consider such a ridiculous proposition," after a horrified glance at another letter.

"Of course not, darling," Mrs. Buckingham said mechanically. "Most unreasonable of them."

"Apart from the fact that you do not know to what I am referring, my dear, I will now make it clear to my assembled family yet once again that anyone who to-day tries to make a living by writing must be considered crazy. He is exploited at every turn and his battle to wrest a living from a hard and unsympathetic public waxes fiercer every day. . . ."

"Yes, darling. We know. But this family likes authors—particularly one author," Juliet said with more than her usual tact. "I don't suppose Simon or me will want to write for a living. . . . You know what I'm going to do, don't you? . . ." and before any of them could answer she jumped up, stepped back a few paces and standing easily flicked back her hair and holding one hand gracefully before her declaimed:

"*All the world's a stage,*
And all the men and women merely players;
They have their exits and their entrances
And one man in his time plays many parts."

"Breakfast, Juliet! Breakfast!" her mother said. "You may find it difficult to believe but even Simon has heard that before."

Juliet curtseyed and flashed a smile at them all before resuming her seat and banging her egg.

After a little Simon thought it was probably safe to introduce the subject which was most on his mind.

"About these holidays," he began tentatively, and had

the grace to look a little abashed when his father and mother stopped eating. " I mean, what *about* them? What are we going to *do* in them? Are we going away somewhere? "

Mr. Buckingham put down his cup.

" You horrify me, Simon. You really do. You sit there on the first day of your holidays and ask what you are going to *do* with them. Have you no ideas? "

" Yes, I have," Simon said just a little too quickly. " I've got lots of ideas! I'd like you to hire a yacht right away while the weather is good and take us all to some islands. . . . I've suddenly gone crazy about islands and I'd like to sail round lots of 'em. . . . And I've got another idea, too. . . ."

" I do not mean that sort of ridiculous and expensive idea," his father broke in coldly. " What I was about to say when you interrupted me was that the modern child has many faults, not the least of which is a lack of initiative and a demand that all his leisure be planned for him. . . . I have spoken to you before on the use of leisure. . . . That will do, Juliet. I am, of course, devoted to you, but there is no need for you to show your affection for me at the breakfast table."

" Yes there is, darling. You're sweet but you're not quite fair about us. I know just what you're going to say next."

Gently but firmly Mr. Buckingham removed his daughter's hand from his head where she was twisting his thinning hair into a tuft.

" When I was your age," he continued loudly enough to drown his children's groans, " When I was your age I made my own adventures. I never troubled my parents by asking on the first day of the holidays, ' What shall

I do?' or, 'What have you arranged for me?' or,
'Please will you hire a yacht and we will go whaling
together.' . . . Juliet, my dear, run and get my cigarettes
and I will make you a suggestion."

When his cigarette was alight he flicked the dead
match into a lavender bush and went on more seriously.

"I was not being fair when I said you had not got
initiative, I know, and I'd like nothing better than to
go sailing as Simon suggests, but I have neither the
money nor the time, and as it will be a few weeks before my book is finished and your mother is the most
devoted and wonderful wife in the world and will not
leave me, I really think you must try and plan something
for yourselves. . . . Now consider for a moment. You
are living in some of the most romantic, beautiful and
exciting country in Britain. Here, we are on the edge
of the Welsh Marches and you both know what that
means. You are not many miles from the unknown and
almost unspoiled Shropshire hill country round Stretton
and a few miles farther west is a rugged range known
as the Stiperstones, crowned by the Devil's Chair which
is said to be older even than the ice age. Through the
country not far from here runs a Roman road and older
still is the great ditch built by the slaves of King Offa
of Mercia to keep out the marauding Welsh. Not far
away is the forgotten little town of Clun in the heart
of hills where, if you are observant and keen enough,
you can still find flint arrow heads. . . . Listen, my
children. My library is full of books and maps. Go and
study them. When you've done that remember that
you've got bicycles and are sound in wind and limb.
The weather is fine, as Simon reminded me, so why
don't you pack up some rucksacks and go off on your

own and have some fun of your own making . . . ? Believe me, young Buckinghams, there is a story behind every front door, the possiblity of adventure in every journey and romance round every corner. . . . If you'll go out and look for these things I believe you'll find them."

"But nothing romantic ever happens to me," Juliet complained. "Every day, even when I go to school, I'm always looking for a real adventure. I'm all keyed up for it, just like I was first thing this morning, but life just passes me by."

She was not really surprised when neither her father nor mother paid any attention to this dramatic outburst and was just searching her mind for a Shakespearian quotation to fit the occasion when she realized that Simon, who was sitting opposite and could see the road over her shoulder, had a gleam of interest in his eye and was struggling to speak through a mouthful of toast. After an anxious gulp he managed to say, "All that stuff is just wasted on us, Sister, but if you really want romance and will look behind you, it's coming right across the common to this very door . . . . Just like Dad said," and he grinned cheekily at his father.

Juliet turned round so abruptly that she upset her chair, but when she picked herself up she was in time to see a good-looking boy of about her own age cycling slowly down the road towards them. There was no doubt, although he was dressed in old clothes, that he was a *very* interesting looking boy, with a lock of dark hair falling over one eye, a tanned face and very white teeth. He was carrying a knapsack on his back and something else which she couldn't recognize was fastened to the back of his bicycle.

Juliet turned to her family with a radiant but wicked smile.

"He's smashing," she whispered. "He's almost an answer to my prayers."

"Juliet!" her mother remonstrated. "Come here at once and behave yourself," and then she added, "But he does look rather romantic, and is that a fiddle fixed to his bicycle? Where can he have come from at this time in the morning?"

Juliet walked across the lawn to the wall and as the stranger came by smiled at him deliberately, while Simon hid his face in his hands and said, "I won't have anything more to do with her. I can't tell you, parents, how ashamed I am."

Mr. Buckingham was watching the proceedings with a twinkle in his eye while his wife blushed a little as Juliet said:

"Hullo. You look a bit lost. Can we help?"

Charles, who had seen the group under the chestnut tree almost as soon as Simon had seen him, wobbled to a stop and smiled at the prettiest girl he had ever seen. In spite of the fact that he had slept only for a few hours in a sandpit he looked fairly fresh and clean, but he was exceedingly hungry and the smell of fresh coffee from the open-air breakfast table made his mouth water. Perhaps he could start earning his living on these nice people? They might want some odd jobs done, although it was hardly the time or place to suggest playing the fiddle. The girl looked fun, too. He glanced at her again and blinked for she certainly was a very pleasant change from Jill and Monica whom he had always disliked for their stiff-necked priggishness. The boy should be all right, too, although he was grinning at his sister like a little monkey.

Then he studied the grown-ups. The lady at the table with her back half to him was obviously the girl's mother. She was small and dainty and looked as if she hadn't a care in the world, and when she turned and smiled at him he saw that her eyes were the same blue as those of the girl. The man, leaning back in his chair with a cigarette smouldering between his fingers, and watching him through half-closed eyes, looked friendly and jolly. There was a humorous quirk to the corners of his mouth and not much hair on the top of his head and very dimly, far at the back of his mind, Charles felt that, if not in appearance, this man was something like his father and that the two men would have liked each other. He was speaking to him now.

" You're out early, my lad. Where have you come from? "

Charles hesitated. He had not yet really considered the question of his identity but it would probably be wiser not to say who he was or where he came from just in case his uncle decided to warn the police. He got off his bicycle, looked faintly embarrassed and then smiled his charming smile.

" I'd rather not say, sir, if you don't mind, but I give you my word that I've done nothing wrong. Honestly I haven't. . . . It's just that I'm paying my way wherever I go and I'd be jolly glad if there were any odd jobs I could do for you. . . . I play the fiddle, too, but maybe breakfast isn't quite the right time for that . . . ."

" Oh yes it is," Juliet said impetuously, and then stopped short as her mother said, " Come inside and have a cup of coffee," while Mr. Buckingham stubbed out his cigarette and with a triumphant " Ha! " repeated the invitation.

" Come in! Come in, my boy. I scent a story here. What did I tell you, Juliet? I am confident that this lad has initiative, courage and resource."

And this was how Charles met the Buckinghams. They all took to each other at once although Simon, perhaps, was a little suspicious for a time. He had just spent some weeks learning from experience that boys only a year or so older than himself are not necessarily as friendly as they appear. He had very good reason —and neither his parents nor his sister were going to be enlightened about this—for distrusting some boys profoundly. He thought more of their visitor, however, when he realized that his upper lip was swollen and split and that he had undoubtedly been fighting not so very long ago.

Charles wheeled his bicycle into the garden, leaned it against the chestnut tree, slipped the knapsack from his shoulders and, with Juliet beside him, advanced on Mrs. Buckingham.

" This is very kind indeed of you," he said. " I may as well confess that I've been sleeping out on the common and if I could have a wash and a cup of coffee maybe I could clean the shoes for you or something like that? "

" Maybe you could. Jolly good idea," Simon said feelingly while Juliet hissed, " Shut up, Simon. He's not going to clean shoes. He's going to play his fiddle to us as soon as he's had something to eat. . . . Come and sit down, stranger, and I'll boil you an egg."

Charles looked at his hands apologetically and Mr. Buckingham said, " Show him the bathroom, Simon," and, as soon as the two boys had gone in, " I suppose he's all right? What do you think? "

" He certainly has charm," Mrs. Buckingham sighed. " You think so too, don't you Julie? "

Her daughter pirouetted across the lawn.

" He's wonderful, of course, and he's got a secret which I'm going to *drag* from him. . . . I'll go and put his egg on."

When Charles came down she said, " We still don't know who you are, but you're going to have breakfast with Mr. and Mrs. Buckingham and their children. My name is Juliet and the little brat who took you upstairs is Simon. . . . What's your name? "

" I know it seems ridiculous," Charles said, " and I'm afraid it's very rude, but will you all please forgive me if I don't tell you my *real* name? . . . You're all very kind to me but I'd appreciate it very much if you wouldn't tell anybody that you've seen me. . . . I promise that I I haven't done anything wrong."

There was a long silence which was broken by Simon.

" Maybe you haven't, but you've been in a good scrap lately. Did you win? "

Charles laughed. " I think so. There were two of them."

" We shall have to call you something," Mrs. Buckingham said as she poured out his coffee. " Sit down here and help yourself to toast. Juliet will bring you an egg in a minute."

Charles flushed.

" I'm sorry, really I am. I know this is very rude but please try and understand. Will you call me John Brown? "

They all laughed at him and Juliet said, " But how

wonderful! Have you just thought of that because your soul goes marching on?"

Charles laughed with them, but Mr. Buckingham noticed a stubborn set about his mouth and stopped the others teasing him.

Charles had never met anyone quite like the Buckinghams. The girl made him laugh by calling him Johnny, and by the time he had finished his breakfast even the boy, who had been watching him suspiciously, was joining in the fun. As for the grown-ups, they just accepted him and treated him as they would do any other guest, and Charles could not help comparing such courtesy with the snobbery of Aunt Mary and his cousins at Manlands.

As soon as he had finished he got up and said to Mrs. Buckingham, "I won't say 'Thank you' again, but please is there any job I could do now to help you— any job in the house or garden I mean?"

Juliet spoke before her mother could answer.

"You see the stone path leading down to the front gate, Johnny? I haven't had time to scrub that yet this morning. Will you scrub it for us?"

While Simon roared with laughter Mrs. Buckingham said:

"Don't take any notice of them, John. They are both behaving very badly. Thank you very much for your offer but I don't think there is anything very special to do this morning. I have some other help coming presently, otherwise I'm quite sure you would have fitted in very nicely with us all."

Mr. Buckingham got up and took out another cigarette.

"I must go and work," he said, and then his eye strayed to the bicycle leaning against the tree. "You can

E

. . . leaning against the chestnut tree, began to play.

play the fiddle can you, boy? If you would really like to do something for us give us a tune now."

"Of course," Charles said happily. "I'd like to play to you all. I'm not very good really, but I hope to be one day, sir."

He unstrapped the case, took out his father's violin, tuned it and, leaning against the chestnut tree, began to play. As the first notes of *Shepherd's Hey* sang across the garden Mrs. Buckingham sat down again while her husband's lighted match burned his fingers. Simon stopped fidgeting and looked at their new friend with real interest and Juliet settled herself on the grass at her mother's feet.

And because Charles sensed at once that they were

all interested and appreciative he needed no second invitation when Juliet said " Go on! Go on! " Soon he forgot everything but his music and it is possible that he had never played better. He played anything and everything that came into his head. After the country dances he played some Mozart and then some sea shanties and once, when he paused and Simon suggested sacrilegiously, " Oh! What a beautiful morning," he grinned at him and played them tunes from *Oklahoma*. Then he became serious again and gave them what Rachmaninoff he could remember, and because this was the music of his father's country he played with a fervour that brought the tears to Juliet's eyes. Then he played an odd little, haunting theme once or twice and lowered his bow.

" Sorry if I've played too much," he murmured. " I forget sometimes. . . . Maybe I'd better be getting on, now."

" That's all right, my boy," Mr. Buckingham said, " Where did you learn to play like that? "

" I think I've always known— " Charles began, and then, " I'm learning now, of course. . . . You see, my father . . ." and he stopped short, turned and began to put his violin back in its case.

" Thank you, John," Mrs. Buckingham added. " Thank you very much. That was a lovely start to the day. I hope you'll come and play for us again— particularly if you don't live too far away."

Before Charles could answer Juliet jumped up and said, " Don't go just yet, Johnny. Come and see the garden."

He hesitated, not sure whether he had outstayed his

welcome. They had been so kind and it had all been such fun that it would be silly to spoil it now.

" *Please,*" Juliet went on. " There's plenty of time and we want to show you something·"

Mrs. Buckingham smiled understandingly.

" I should see the garden before you go, John. Perhaps you could help those two feed the chickens? That's a job Simon always dodges if he can."

Charles put down the violin case.

" Thank you very much," he said. " I haven't got to go for a few minutes," and followed Juliet and Simon.

As soon as they were out of earshot the former stopped under an apple tree. She turned to Charles, and because he was a few inches taller, had to look up at him as she spoke.

" Now listen to me, Johnny Brown, and don't you interrupt, Simon, until I've finished. . . . Now, Johnny. We Buckinghams are quite good at minding our own business 'cos we're rather a family and we stick together and have lots of fun of our own. I'm telling you this because we don't want to butt in and interfere with you unless you want us to. . . . No! You needn't say anything now. . . . Wait till I've finished. . . . I haven't spoken to Simon yet—not by ourselves I mean—but I think you've run away from home for some reason that is nothing to do with us—please don't interrupt—and that you don't quite know where you're going or what you're going to do. . . . We don't even know whether you're being chased or whether you've got to hide, but if you really are off somewhere on your own then I think Simon and me would like to join up with you.—No, don't say anything yet, Johnny, and you keep quiet too, Simon. I know what you're thinking. . . . I was going to tell you that our parents were just telling us when you arrived that we never planned anything on our own nor had any holidays that weren't organized by grown-ups. . . . Well, Johnny, if you'd like us to come with you for a bit we will. We've got bikes. What do you think? "

" I'd like it," Charles said without hesitation. " What do you think of it, young Simon? "

" All right," the younger boy agreed. " I don't see why not. Julie gets very excited sometimes but you'll find she's all right—for a girl I mean· . . . When shall we start? "

" That's good! " Charles said. " And thanks very much for asking me, but you don't know anything about me, do you? "

" Not yet," Juliet agreed, " but I soon shall. You won't be able to keep any secrets from me. . . . Now listen to my idea. . . . Do you know Ludlow, Johnny? It's about six miles from here."

" I was trying to get there but I lost my way in the night."

" Good. It's nearly nine o'clock now. Simon and I will have to tidy up here first and pack our haversacks, so let's meet at the top of the Keep of Ludlow Castle at eleven o'clock. You'll be there first, Johnny, but you'll wait for us won't you? The snag is that you have to pay to go in but its a wonderfully romantic place to meet."

" I think it's a stupid idea," Simon said, " but there won't be many other people up there at that time in the morning. . . . I'd rather meet in that café where the ices are so good."

" I remember that place," Charles agreed, " but let's

meet where Juliet suggests. I've only been up there once."

" All right. Eleven o'clock then," Juliet said excitedly. "We'll make a solemn pact and like the Three Musketeers we'll stick together through thick and thin. . . . But we mustn't have any secrets between us. You'll have to tell us something about yourself, Johnny! "

Charles looked uneasy.

" You'll have to trust me. It is true that I've run away from the only home I've got because I've had a row with my two cousins while my mother is in Switzerland. I ought to tell you that my uncle may tell the police that I've run away and that I'll be chased. Maybe they're searching for me now although I haven't done anything wrong, but even if they are I'm not going back until I've proved that I can make my own way. It will be grand if you'll join up with me for a while, but I warn you that I don't know where I'm going or what I'm going to do. Please don't ask me any more questions now."

" That's all right," Simon said. " I like this idea better and better. Don't take too much notice of my sister. She's always acting and she's horribly nosy by nature."

Juliet pushed him aside.

" I think this is wonderful, Johnny. This really is going to be an adventure. We'll come with you and maybe the enemy won't be likely to trace you if we all three stick together and look like a family. The parents can't stop us because they were saying just now that we can't make our own adventures. We'll trust you if you'll trust us, but I'm wondering whether it would be wiser after all for you to wait for us here so that we go to Ludlow together. Do you think the police will be watching for you yet? "

" I don't think so. I don't believe Uncle will do anything in a hurry and I know he'll hate to let anyone
know I've run away. He's very respectable."

" How perfectly awful for you," Juliet replied. " I
should hate really respectable parents. Ours are
wonderful."

" I'm sure they are. I can see that. They've been
wonderful to me, too. . . . I'll go and say ' Good-bye '
to them now and see you later. . . . And, thank you both
very much for being so decent to me."

In the embarrassed silence which followed Simon
looked shocked at such a display of emotion, while Juliet
flushed and glanced vaguely up into the apple tree.

Then, " That's settled," she said brightly. " You get
off now and we'll break the news to the parents after
you've gone."

The grown-ups came out to the gate to see him off.
There was no doubt that his manners were charming,
but Mrs. Buckingham watched him with a twinkle in
her eye as he cycled off.

" I can't believe that he's as wonderful as he looks,"
she said and Mr. Buckingham added:

" Now that we've bid Godspeed to our latest visitor
perhaps I may be allowed to retire and get on with my
work."

" Not for a minute, Daddy, please," Juliet pleaded.
" We've got something very important indeed to tell you
both. We've come to a great decision."

" We're following your advice, Dad. That's all,"
Simon grinned. " We're going off to find our own
adventures."

" I can spare you five minutes," their father said.
" Tell us all."

There wasn't really much to tell but they admitted that the sudden appearance of John Brown had influenced them, but they were a little surprised at their mother's answer when Juliet said, " The weather's fine and we'll take macks. You don't mind, do you? "

" I don't mind at all," she said. " I expect you'll do all sorts of stupid things and the experience will be very good for you. But do be careful of that wonderful young man."

" He's all right, Mummy, really he is. I'm sure of it. I think he's got a secret in his life and just for a few days anyway we're going out to find some adventures together. You know we'll be sensible."

Mr. Buckingham passed his daughter two one pound notes.

" Don't be too sensible, my dear. You'll have no fun if you are, but never forget what we've tried to show you here. Think before you speak and when you meet strangers listen more than you talk. . . . Here are your iron rations, but if you'll take my advice you'll only spend them if you've got to do so. . . . Earn as you go, if you can."

Juliet hugged him while Simon said, " You're wonderful parents. I mean—you don't seem to worry much about this. Don't you even care where we sleep, Mother? "

" Not really. You'll learn to appreciate your own beds all the more. . . . I agree with your father, darlings, but you must promise to ring up if either of you are ill, or in trouble, or are really stranded for want of money. It won't hurt you to sleep out in this weather if you take your sweaters, but it won't be fun if it's wet. . . .

Oh! And if you're going to be away a long time you might send us a post card."

" Good-bye, then," Mr. Buckingham said. " May I go and work now? "

" Just one thing, Dad," Simon said. " If, by some awful chance, some person called here after we've gone and asked if you'd seen a boy called John Brown round these parts you wouldn't have, would you? "

" I deplore your misuse of the English language, my boy, but I think I could truthfully deny what you suggest. . . . I feel quite sure that John Brown is not his name. . . . Be off with you."

And he winked at them solemnly.

CHAPTER 4

MARYKNOLL

THERE is no other place in England quite like Ludlow. In the twelfth century it was a walled town with seven gates, of which only one now remains, but everything else about it to-day is overshadowed by its magnificent castle, a memorial to the days when its courtyards echoed to the ring of steel on steel, and armour-clad knights rode over its drawbridge to fight the marauding Welsh.

Ludlow is seen at its best if approached from the South or West, and although Juliet and Simon knew every inch of their road, they were rarely too preoccupied to appreciate what they saw. They knew and loved the outline of Clee Hill standing high above the town on the English side and, when they came home from school, looked for the sun lighting up the bare face of the quarries almost at the summit. On the other side of the town and running away to the West towards Wales was a range of seven smaller hills, each with its clump of trees on the top. They had often bathed in the flashing waters of the lovely Teme below the castle and Simon, while the craze lasted, had once spent a lot of time at the railway station collecting the numbers of the engines and making friends with the signalman. They knew the big church of St. Lawrence too, and the fascinating little bookshop in Broad Street and the cafés.

It was nearly eleven as they rode over Ludford Bridge and jumped off their cycles at the foot of the steep hill leading up to Broad Gate. The sun was already hot and

74

it seemed as if the inhabitants of Ludlow had determined
not to exert themselves until the cool of the evening,
for only a few people were about. A cat drowsed beside
some geraniums in a window-box and hardly opened an
eye as a puppy on the pavement below set up a frenzied
yapping. A baker's van rattled through the old gateway
and the driver, who had a rose stuck in his cap, winked
boldly at Juliet who was just saying:

"I wonder if Johnny has been here long, Simon.
You did believe what he said, didn't you? I'm not sure
that Mother did."

"He's all right," her brother answered. "I think he's
a bit *peculiar*. I'm not quite sure what it is, but somehow
he's not like other chaps at school. Maybe he's not all
English if you know what I mean. All the same I
like him very much. . . . Why did you say we'd meet
him at the top of the keep? You couldn't have thought
of anywhere farther off or more difficult. . . . I think
I'll wait down here and have an ice and you can climb
those millions of stone steps and fetch him down. . . .
I couldn't help thinking he was a bit dumb to agree to
such a silly idea."

"It isn't a silly idea at all," Juliet protested. "We
agreed to make a pact to stick together and that's a
solemn thing to do and we ought to do it in a solemn
place."

"I don't mind making a pact while I'm eating an
ice—so long as it's a decent ice. I can't see the sense
of paying to climb up a lot of stairs just to meet a chap
with a fiddle who says his name is John Brown when
it isn't. . . . Who's that ghastly looking girl?"

Juliet, who had been smiling "Hullo" at a girl in
a green blazer who obviously wanted to stop for a chat,

answered briefly, " I've forgotten her name but I think it's Muriel. I can't stand her."

" Good," said Simon. " Neither can I. Let's grin at everyone we meet like that and then we'll get on really quickly. . . . If Johnny isn't at the top of the tower when we get there I shall pursue him all over the country until I find him and then force him to pay me back my entrance money. It's wicked to make people pay to go into a ruin that they've seen before."

As this was almost feminine logic Juliet merely looked at her brother affectionately. " You're a silly little boy," she said. " We're going to have fun, Simon. I know we are. We haven't had a real adventure for years."

At the top of the hill they turned to the left into Castle Street and left their bicycles leaning against the Gateway Tower.

" I refuse to haul my haversack up to the top," Simon said. " Let's ask the man who takes the money to keep them for us."

There was no difficulty about this and as they strolled across the grassy forecourt and crossed the two-arched stone bridge, which has taken the place of the old draw-bridge, Simon was whistling cheerfully.

Juliet, as she had so often done before, was trying to imagine how the courtyard would have looked when crowded with caparisoned horses and armoured men carrying lances with streaming pennants. On the bridge she glanced back at the great tower in the corner of the outer courtyard, thinking how wonderful it would have been to be a woman in those brave days and watch from the battlements your lover, with your favour in his helmet, ride out to battle.

" Do buck up," Simon said impatiently. " You look

moonstruck or something. Let's go and find this chap
and then have a good rest and an ice."

"You ought to pay more attention to places like this,"
Juliet remonstrated solemnly. "This is holy ground. . . .
Did you know that Milton's *Comus* was first played in
the big hall in this castle? . . . But of course you're too
young to know what that was. Have you ever heard
of *Comus*, little man?"

"I'll say I have if you promise not to recite any of
it," her brother said rudely. "Come on, Julie."

They turned through a narrow doorway, into the keep
and began to climb the slippery, narrow steps. From floor
to floor they clambered in single file until they reached
the top which was caged in with iron bars. Juliet was
in front and was too breathless to answer Charles'
"Hullo, you two. I was sure you'd come. Is everything
all right? . . You're out of training, Juliet?"

"That's all very well," she gasped with her hand to
her side, "but I bet you were as puffed when you came
up. You've been up here for ages."

"Did you cycle up?" Simon asked cheekily. "Now
let's have our council of war as soon as we can and get
down again."

"I'm glad you suggested this place," Charles said to
Juliet. "It's grand. I've been here once before but it
was misty and we couldn't see very far."

They stood in silence for a few minutes gazing out
across the wonderful panorama of the summer countryside. To the North-East stretched the straight ridge of
Wenlock Edge, and far to the North, bounding the
chequered plain through the midst of which the railway ran, were the blue shadows of the Stretton Hills.
To the West were the seven little hills crowned with

trees, and to the South, almost at their feet, the sparkling Teme swept round the edge of the cliff on its way to join the mighty Severn.

Suddenly and unaccountably, they all seemed a little shy of each other and it was a relief when Juliet said, " Well. What do we do now? "

Charles pushed back the wayward lock of hair.

" Before we do anything are you two sure that you really want to join up with me? I'll understand perfectly if you've had enough and like to clear off on your own. . . . I know you don't believe my name is John Brown, and there's not much more I can really tell you. . . . There's no particular reason why you should believe me or trust me, and I do understand that."

" Is that all? " Simon asked.

" More or less, but I do want you to understand that if you stick with me you may get into real trouble. . . . It may not be fun for you at all and you've been so decent to me."

" All right, Johnny. All right! " Juliet said quickly. " Please don't start all that ' decent ' business again. . . . Don't you remember that I told you not long ago we'd all make a pact to stick together and you agreed? You can't get out of it now, and if you would we won't let you go, so you'd better forget the idea of doing all this by yourself. . . . By the way, what *are* you going to do, Johnny? Have you thought exactly how you're going to make yourself independent? "

" I haven't thought about it much. I hoped I'd earn a shilling or two by the Scouts' ' Bob-a-Job ' idea, and then, of course, I can always play my fiddle and people may throw me pennies."

" They won't always, I bet," Simon said. " Anyway

you can't drift round the streets waiting for something to turn up. If the police do begin to look for you they'll look in towns first. . . . It's a horrible thought, but I suppose we shall all three have to find separate jobs in a place like this. I don't mind telling you two that I hate the idea of even beginning to earn a living. . . . Maybe I could get a job with a farmer to keep the birds off his fields. I could rest a lot of the time."

"Simon is right, Johnny. I'm sure it's not wise to stay in Ludlow too long," Juliet replied. "What we really want is a circus or a fair. Not only would lovely people like that keep you away from the police, but perhaps we could live with them for a bit in a caravan. We could persuade them to put on our own act. . . ."

"*Our* act?" Charles interrupted. "What do you mean?"

"We'll make up an act and do it together—all three of us, although I'm not quite sure what Simon will do?"

"And what do you do?" Charles asked coldly.

"Me?" Juliet flushed. "But of course you don't know yet. How could you? I'm going to be an actress as soon as I'm old enough."

"She's jolly good," Simon confirmed unexpectedly. "And I think this is a fine idea."

"Well anyway," Juliet went on, "I'll try and make myself beautiful and recite. I'll do something that my namesake said. . . . Perhaps you and I could do Romeo and Juliet together, Johnny whatever-your-name-is," she added generously.

"I don't think I'd be much good at that," Charles said hastily, "But of course I can play my fiddle anywhere at any time, and that ought to keep us going for a bit. . . . What about young Simon?"

" I wish you wouldn't keep on calling me *young* Simon. I have to remember I'm not very old while I'm away at school and I'm sick of it. . . . If you mean what I am going to do next the answer is easy—I'm going down into the town to get an ice. When that's over I think we ought all to try and earn some money by doing jobs like the Boy Scouts did and that should earn us enough to get some lunch. After that we'd better arrange to meet somewhere and then we can go off into the country and find a place to eat again and sleep." . . . Then, when he noticed the other two watching him with admiration, he added, " And I don't think it's a good idea to play your fiddle about Ludlow, Johnny. I know you might get more money quickly, but there are too many people about and everybody would be talking about you. . . . If you and Julie are going to put on a performance it had better not be here. . . . Come on. Let's go down."

As they recrossed the great courtyard more than one party of visitors turned for a second glance at the good-looking youngsters talking so animatedly. Simon, who was much shrewder than most people suspected and was prepared to take this adventure seriously, was aware that his sister and their new friend were good-looking and unusual enough to be remembered. He was certain that they ought to separate for a while. It might even be better to leave Ludlow at once.

The other two were just in front. Johnny, striding easily with his hands in the pockets of his corduroys, was laughing at something which Juliet was saying. They made a striking contrast—the one so dark and the girl so fair; the boy in ordinary drab clothes and Juliet, slim, lively, with brown, bare legs, gleaming hair and the bright blue blouse she loved to wear. Maybe they could put on an act together, Simon thought without envy. They might be good. . . . Or his sister would be anyway.

He caught them up at the gateway.

" We must buy a map," he said. " I forgot to bring one."

" I've got one," Charles smiled. " Let's go and get ices and study it. I left my bike and haversack with a chap just here who keeps a shop. I'll run on and get the map, but you might leave your bikes and luggage here as well until we go off this afternoon."

Ten minutes later one dark, one fair and one medium-coloured, but tousled head, were bent over the map in a corner of the café of Simon's choice. The ices had come and gone and because the restaurant was filling up they spoke in lowered voices.

" We know all this country fairly well," Juliet was saying, " and there are lots of ways we could go. . . . This side of Wenlock Edge is Corve Dale. Easy cycling and lovely villages. If we go farther north along the main road we go through Onibury towards Craven Arms. I believe that's not very far from a little place called Clun which Daddy told us once was rather exciting. . . . But haven't you any ideas yourself, Johnny? If you would tell us a little more about yourself and where you've come from and how long you think you're going to be able to keep this up, it would make it easier for us."

" I'm sorry," Charles muttered. " Maybe I will tell you soon, but not here and now. As to where we go presently, I think we ought to keep away from main roads but try and find a farm and a haystack where we

F

could sleep. . . . Let's look at the map again. There's a splodge of green over on the left here to the west. That looks lonely enough with plenty of woods, too."

Juliet pulled the map towards her while Simon jingled some loose change in his pocket, wondering whether he dare order another ice.

"We know that," Juliet said. "That big hill is High Vinalls and the valley with the stream is called Mary Knowle. There's a story about that but I've forgotten it except that there must once have been a shrine to the Virgin Mary up by the road. Mother told me that the valley is really the 'adventurous glade' in *Comus* which was acted in the castle. I've read it once. Some of the words are lovely."

"Are there many farms and houses up that way or is it as lonely as it looks?"

"There's a road leading to a tiny place called Aston, but we could camp in the woods to-night if we can't find a farmer who will lend us his barn."

Simon, in the cause of economy, now abandoned the idea of another ice and broke into the conversation.

"We'd better split up now and try and earn some money. If we don't get enough to buy a good meal I'm going home again."

"Simon! You miserable little misery!" Juliet said indignantly. "You can't go home, and anyway your haversack is stuffed with sandwiches and fruit."

"Those are my lunch," he grinned. "Come on! Let's meet at the shop where we left our bikes at three o'clock and then start off for the Mary Knowle woods. I'm not going to tell you two what I'm going to do else you might steal the idea. . . . Cheerio!" and he wandered out into the sunshine.

" That young brother of yours is a bit cocky," Charles remarked as he got up. " Before we know where we are he'll be ordering us about."

" He knows his own mind, anyway," Juliet laughed. " I don't take too much notice of him."

" Yes you do. You both stick up for each other all the time. It must be fun to have a brother—or a sister for that matter. I've only got two pimply cousins."

" You must tell me about them sometime ! . . . Good luck, Johnny. Let's see how we get on, but don't get yourself noticed too much just in case."

" Maybe we'd better try and do something together? " Charles suggested, not feeling so keen on independent action as he had been some hours ago.

Juliet smiled at him over her shoulder as she went out. " Three o'clock. Don't be late."

Charles was the first to reach the rendezvous. He was feeling rather pleased with himself for he had made six shillings by acting as errand boy to an ironmonger. He felt that the money had been well earned for he had made several very difficult journeys up steep hills on a heavy bicycle which was too big for him.

Juliet arrived next and she seemed to have lost some of her early morning sparkle, although she tried a bright and rather artificial smile as soon as she saw Charles leaning against the shop window.

" Hullo ! " he greeted her. " How much? "

" Five bob. I'm worn out. I've been washing-up. I went back to that café and asked if they wanted another waitress, and all they could suggest was the sink. It was foul ! I've washed up millions of greasy plates, and coffee cups full of cigarette ash. . . . Let's get out of this town. I'm sick of it. . . . Where's Simon? "

" He's coming up the street and looks suspiciously fresh to me. He's not hurrying either."

Simon smiled at them both condescendingly.

" You both look fagged out. Have you got much? I do hope so because I've only made sixpence. I don't think I'm awfully good at this. Maybe I've got a lot to learn."

" What have you been doing? " Juliet demanded through clenched teeth.

Simon dodged into the gutter.

" Not much," he admitted. " I bought two pies in a shop by the castle and then I went down to the river. The sun was hot and I sat down because I was tired and it was after two when I woke up. It was a bit late to start work then so when I saw a man coming out of a house I opened the door of his car for him and he thought I was mad and gave me sixpence. . . . And now here I am, but you needn't tell me what you've been doing if you don't want to."

" It's no use getting furious with him, Johnny. We'll get our own back. Now let's get the bikes and be off."

Charles hated the idea of cycling but they were away in ten minutes, after buying some more food and fruit. Several cars passed them on the road and Juliet remarked that most of the occupants looked rather dressed up.

" I think there's a big party on somewhere," Simon said and then, when neither of them answered he added, " And there's no need for you both to be sulky," but all the same he was rather ashamed of himself.

Before long they had to dismount and walk, for the road was steep, and it was soon after Juliet had pointed out the valley of Mary Knowle on their left that they came to the entry to a little lane on the opposite side

of the road. The blast of a horn behind them made
them jump to one side and then a large car turned
into the lane.

" There's something going on round here," Juliet said.
" I suggest we go down and have a look. . . . Lots of
cars have been this way. Look at the tyre marks in the
dust. Did you see that woman in the back of that car?
She was wearing the most revolting hat I've ever seen."

Charles looked at her with new respect. He was not
very observant himself and seemed surprised that anyone
else should be. He was also tired and very saddle sore,
and welcomed any suggestion that would enable him
to forget his bicycle for a while. Simon, for once, had
nothing to say and followed the other two meekly.

Three hundred yards down the lane they came to the
entrance to a big house. The double gates of wrought
iron which were set in a high holly hedge were wide
open and just inside, at the edge of the gravelled drive,
a man was sitting at a small table. From the gardens
behind him came the hum of many voices.

" So here's the party," Juliet said as she jumped off
her bike. " Let's go in for a bit."

" Perhaps it's private? " Charles wondered. " It's a
long way for people to come to a garden party."

" You see that man with the foxy nose sitting at the
table? " Simon said. " I don't like him."

" He's there to take money," Juliet protested. " I can
see a roll of tickets. Of course we can go in. I'll go
and ask him. . . . Hold my bike, Johnny."

She flicked back her hair and sauntered over. It was
true that the guardian of the gate was not very pre-
possessing. He was thin, with a freckled face, pointed
nose and sandy coloured hair. Behind rimless glasses

his eyes were pale and when Juliet smiled at him he looked away.

"Good afternoon. We're on a cycling holiday. Could you please tell me where we are?"

His voice was as unpleasant as his appearance.

"This is the private residence of Mr. Septimus Bland and is known as Maryknoll. You are approximately a quarter of a mile from the road to Ludlow which is three miles distant. . . . Kindly move away from the gateway and do not impede the traffic."

Juliet turned to the others.

"Out of the way, chaps. Mind the traffic." Then, "Thank you very much. Is Mr. Bland having a party in aid of something?"

"Once a year Mr. Bland is kind enough to place his house and garden at the disposal of a committee of distinguished people who work to raise funds for a worthy cause."

The boys came over and leaned the bicycles against the gates.

"Are they trying to raise money this afternoon?" Charles asked. "Because if they are I might be able to help."

The foxy man's face was deepening in colour.

"Go away," he barked. "Take those bicycles away. . . . This flower show is an important social event."

"How my Aunt Mary would love it," Charles grinned. "I only hope she's not here," and when Juliet looked at him suspiciously he added, "She wouldn't be, of course, but she is very social. . . . Let's go in, shall we? . . . How much is it? We can park our bikes somewhere I suppose?"

Foxy began to argue and Charles' temper to rise, and

" These children, sir. They're in the way with their bicycles and now they want to come in."

they were both shouting at each other when a pleasant looking elderly man in a light alpaca suit and a panama hat strolled down the drive towards them.

" Now, Simmonds," he said in a soft, pleasant voice. " What is all this commotion about if you please? "

Juliet, who was rather amused at Charles' outburst, looked up with interest. There was a touch of authority in the newcomer's voice which suggested that he might well be Mr. Septimus Bland, but he looked kind and there was surely a twinkle behind his spectacles as she caught his eye and smiled.

" These children, sir. They're in the way with their bicycles and now they want to come in."

" We can pay, sir," Simon said unexpectedly.

" I'm sure you can, young man, and we shall be very pleased to take your money. The fête is in aid of our new Village Hall and you, my boy, being the youngest of the three, will be admitted for ninepence instead of one and sixpence."

Juliet, who had been wondering of whom Mr. Bland reminded her, now decided that it was certainly Mr. Pickwick, except that he was not quite as plump and wore horn-rimmed glasses instead of the funny little spectacles which had always fascinated her in the illustrations to *Pickwick Papers*.

" You must be Mr. Bland," she said. " We'd like to see your flower show. May we hide our bikes and haversacks somewhere and come and look round? . . . You pay for me, Johnny, and I'll pay you back. Simon can pay for himself as he earned sixpence this afternoon," and she swept past the sandy Simmonds with her head in the air.

Mr. Bland seemed amused by them and Charles noticed that more than once he glanced at the violin case on his bicycle as he led them up the drive.

" The cars are parked in a field which can be reached through that gate," he said, as he pointed out a track leading through the trees. " You can leave your bicycles and luggage there. I trust you will enjoy yourselves. Good afternoon," and he raised his hat to Juliet politely and walked away. Then he stopped, turned and addressed himself to Charles.

" You have a violin there, my boy. Do you play yourself? "

" Yes, sir. I'm very keen."

" You must be if you carry it round with you," Mr. Bland smiled. " Very good, my boy! Splendid! Keep it up. I like to see the new generation interested in music-making."

"Funny old boy," Simon said when he was out of earshot. "Let's get these bikes parked somewhere and then have a look round. I'm getting hungry again, but I expect they do teas in here."

"I think he's a lovely old man," Juliet said. "But p'raps he's not so very old after all. He soon put that foxy man at the gate in his place."

Maryknoll was a gracious, Georgian house in a perfect setting, standing on a gentle rise above lawns and flower borders which sloped down to a stream. A mighty cedar tree before the house towered almost to its roof, and everywhere a great crowd of people thronged over the grass and round the tents and sideshows. The Buckinghams were used to local flower shows, but Charles was not, and as he was anxious not to show his ignorance he kept rather quiet as, with Juliet at his side, they gently elbowed their way towards the biggest marquee. Simon proved rather a trial and they were waiting for him while he tried to drop a few pennies over a sixpence at the bottom of a pail of water when an elderly lady, wearing a most unsuitable hat festooned with flowing ribbons, swooped down on Juliet.

"Now, my dear," she twittered, "This is just the very thing for you. All you have to do is to guess the number of beans in this pretty glass jar and if you are right you will get a big, big prize. . . . This is just the very thing for little schoolgirls. . . . Only sixpence a guess. . . . How many tickets would you like?"

Juliet looked at her coldly and when Charles grinned and said, "Do you think she's old enough to try? Shouldn't she be allowed to have a shot at half-price?"

she raised her sandalled foot and kicked him sharply on the ankle.

"It wouldn't be fair for me to try," she said with a winning smile. "It was my mummy put the beans in the ickle pot and I tounted them up after breakfast."

"That was very wrong of you," Charles said as they walked away, "Very wrong, and not truthful either. I'm ashamed of you."

It was while the three of them were jammed in the big tent against the exhibit of flower decorations that Juliet said to Charles, "That's about the hundredth time you've nearly maimed me with that fiddle of yours. I can't think why you brought it into the show." . . . Then she paused. "But of course I know why you've brought it. This is the very place to make some money for us and for Mr. Bland too. We'll put on an act. You'll have to play and I'm going to recite. . . . Shut up, Simon. Stop poking me like that—Oh! I'm *so* sorry," she said to a handsome young man behind her who was trying in vain to get to his cigarette case. "I'm *so* sorry. I thought you were my brother."

He gave her a friendly grin and her cheeks were rather pink as she turned back to Charles. "Anyway," she maintained, "I'm going to recite and I bet they'll like it. I've heard you play, Johnny, and I think you're wonderful, but honestly I'm not too bad. . . . Let's get out of this and find Mr. Bland. We shall have to ask his permission. . . . Oh, here you are, Simon. . . . Come on! You'll have to collect the money."

Charles was soon infected by her enthusiasm, and by some skilful infiltration by Simon they forced their way outside. Mr. Bland was discovered under the cedar tree almost entirely surrounded by gracious ladies.

" I bet there's not a Mrs. Bland," Juliet whispered shrewdly, " He's very popular, isn't he? Leave this to me."

After a little she caught his eye and smiled. His response was not quite what she had expected for he looked away pretending not to have seen her. But the lady to whom he was speaking noticed and said something which the children could not hear.

Juliet took a chance and stepped forward.

" Do please forgive me for interrupting, Mr. Bland, but you were very kind to us just now at the gate, and as we've got an idea which we think might help your wonderful show, we thought we'd like to ask your advice—and all these ladies' too—and get your permission to do it."

" Charming child," one of the ladies murmured. " Nice manners and pretty too."

" The boy with the violin looks exceptional," her companion replied. " Who are they? "

Mr. Bland, wisely taking up his cue, beamed on them benevolently.

" Do not keep us in suspense," he begged. " Come and tell us who you are and what you want to do."

Juliet explained. " This is my brother, Simon and I'm Juliet Buckingham. This is our great friend, John Brown, and we're having a holiday on bikes together, but we're trying to pay our way as we go. We've earned a few shillings to-day and had lots of fun, and if we can't afford to sleep in beds somewhere to-night we shall sleep under a haystack or in a barn. . . . But this is the point. Johnny here plays the violin wonderfully and I'm going to be an actress one day and I learn elocution and I know lots of things. . . . Please, Mr. Bland, may we give a performance together here? Simon can take a collection—he's jolly good at that sort of thing—if we did well p'raps you'd let us keep a little of the money to help us on our way? "

Some of them laughed at her but not Mr. Bland, who turned to Charles and said, " Can you really play the fiddle? "

" I told you, sir, that I'm learning all the time, but if you like I'll show you now what I can do," and before they could stop him the violin was out of its case and under his chin. He gave them the Mozart which he had played at Leasend only a few hours ago, and when he lowered his bow there was a long pause before Mr. Bland said, " Very interesting. You and I must have a talk sometime, Master Brown. . . . I think you ladies will agree that the idea of these youngsters is excellent. . . . Come with me and we will find you a suitable pitch."

Instantly Juliet's mouth went dry, her knees shook and she felt sick with excitement. It was one thing to say she was going to be an actress and that she could recite, but a very different thing to be faced with such an eventuality within a few minutes. They were all moving out of the shade of the cedar now and a jolly, plump woman was saying to her, " Where do you come from, Juliet? I like your idea very much and you spoke out well. What are you going to recite? "

Juliet gulped. " I'm not sure yet. I wish I hadn't offered. Johnny had better do everything by himself."

The stranger lowered her voice. " I shouldn't let him do that, my dear—I don't think it would be good for him. . . . Good luck. . . . I was on the stage before I married," and she moved away.

Charles came over and took hold of her arm.

" We're for it now, Juliet. Will you start first? "

" I feel sick, Johnny. I can't face it. I don't know what I'm going to do and I can't remember a word of anything."

" I don't believe you," Charles replied, and indeed he could not understand how anybody could be nervous about performing in public. True, he always felt excited and worked up, but never afraid.

Mr. Bland led them between the crowds and through a wrought iron gate into a lovely, sunk garden. At the far end, in an alcove in a yew hedge, was a long stone seat with a paved terrace in front of it.

" There you are, my children. An ideal place for a pastoral performance. For you, young lady, it may be the Forest of Arden or perhaps Titania's glade. . . . And you, my young genius, will doubtless make music to fit the occasion and the surroundings. Stay here until we bring you an audience worthy of your powers."

Then they were alone in the sunk garden with the scent of lavender and late roses blowing about them and the tinkle of water from a little fountain the only sound, until Simon said:

" Now you've done it. I'm jolly glad I've only got to collect the money."

Juliet watched Charles as he took out his violin and suddenly made up her mind that she was going through with this. But what should she do? Not Portia, certainly, and of course she would never dare to do Ophelia. " Forest of Arden " he had said, but could she remember Rosalind? Wouldn't it be better not to do Shakespeare? Perhaps the scene from Shaw's *St. Joan* where the Maid recants and tears up her confession. Her lips moved silently as she tried to remember the words:

" Yes: they told me you were fools and that I was not to listen to your fine words nor trust to your charity. You promised me my life but you lied. You think that life is nothing but being stone dead. . . ."

Did she dare? Joan, when she had spoken these words, was not, perhaps, so very many years older. Juliet knew that this was no part for a schoolgirl but she could see the scene now. See Joan on her little stool with the Inquisitors around her and she was certain the words would came back. Or should she do Perdita's song of the flowers?

She did both, for almost before she had made up her mind Mr. Bland came back and in a few minutes the sunken garden was full of laughing, chattering, curious guests. She did not hear the words of his little speech for the thudding of her heart, but suddenly there was a hush, then a burst of clapping and Charles' voice just behind her.

" Good luck, Julie. Go to it."

The faces before her were blurred and wavering, but suddenly she picked out the lady who had been an actress and the nice, brown young man who had smiled at her in the flower-show tent. His smile now was friendly and encouraging.

She stepped forward and her voice shook pitifully as she announced, " A scene from Bernard Shaw's *St. Joan*."

She sat on the edge of the stone seat. The words came back.

" Perpetual imprisonment! Am I not then to be set free? " and after the final words, *" I know that your*

counsel is of the devil, and that mine is of God," there was a burst of applause. The Court of the Inquisitors faded and she saw the sunken garden again. She smiled, curtsied and, overcome with sudden shyness, squeezed back against the hard yew hedge.

" That was grand, Julie," Charles was saying. " Sorry, I didn't know you were so good. . . . Go back again. They want another."

She caught the eye of the actress who was still clapping and at her nod of encouragement went back to the seat. It was easier this time.

" I would I had some flowers o' the spring that might become your time of day," she began.

Then Charles played and he knew that he had never played better. Again and again the friendly audience encored him, until at last he admitted that he could do no more without music. Mr. Bland made another little speech and Simon, with his eyes almost popping out of his head with excitement, watched the notes as well as silver tossed into the hat he was holding.

Now Mr. Bland was very gracious and almost purred over them.

" An excellent performance, my dear," he said as he patted Juliet with a pudgy hand. " You show great promise. Come back to the house and have some refreshment." But he was more interested in Charles, for having acknowledged Juliet's efforts he wasted no further time on her.

" I am extremely interested in your music, my boy. I happen to be something of a musician myself and I should like you to play again for me. . . . May I examine your instrument? It possesses a very remarkable tone."

They were on the terrace now outside the french

windows of a drawing-room, the main furnishing of which seemed to be a white grand piano.

Rather reluctantly Charles passed the fiddle over. He was hoping that he would not be asked too many awkward questions for he knew it would never do for him to admit his real identity.

Mr. Bland was over five minutes examining the violin. He took it inside and with his back to the children, switched on a lamp on the piano, turning the violin over and over in his hands. When at last he came back to the window, Simon said, " What about all this money, sir, and did you say something about refreshments? "

" Yes, yes, my boy. Later! Later! " Mr. Bland almost snapped, then to Charles, " I should like you to come back to supper with me at eight o'clock and we might make some music together. Will you come back later, boy, when this show is over? I think you said that you are on holiday? "

" Thank you very much, sir, but I can't do that. I'm with my friends here, you see."

" I meant all of you, of course," Mr. Bland corrected himself. " Come back at eight o'clock sharp. You can leave your fiddle here. I will take care of it."

Charles stepped forward and took the violin. " I'm sorry, sir. I couldn't do that."

" Stay here, then," the man suggested. " Stop and play some more before the people go, have some supper with me and your friends can come back for you later —say between nine thirty and ten o'clock. That will be best."

Charles shook his head and Mr. Bland took his arm and led him into the room and whispered to him. Poor Juliet, now feeling a reaction from the afternoon's excitement and furious at the favouritism being shown to their friend, had tears in her eyes when Charles came back alone.

"Listen," he whispered. "The old boy's crazy, but when I said I wouldn't stay without you he said he'd give me a pound if I would. . . . He says it's just me that he wants although he likes you very much. I don't want to stay, Juliet. Honestly I don't, but a pound will help to make us independent. What do you think?"

At first Juliet was sure that the right thing to do was to fling the money in Mr. Bland's face, but then she realized that a pound was not so easily earned and that with it they needn't, perhaps, sleep under a haystack. A bath would be nice, too, and maybe they could find some woman with lodgings to let in a nearby village. Then Simon, who was getting very bored, said, "You stay, John, and we'll come back for you later. You earn the money. It will be useful and save me holding open car doors. I hated doing that. It could be quite exhausting."

Juliet nodded. "All right. I think he's a rude old man, but it is easy money."

"Don't go too far away, Juliet, and I'm trusting you both to find somewhere for us to spend the night. With this money—and we've got our share of the collection too—we'll be living in luxury." . . . He turned and called Mr. Bland. "Thank you very much, sir. I'll stay and play again as you so kindly suggested, and my friends will go and find somewhere to sleep and come back at half-past nine. . . . May we take our share of the collection, please? You did promise that, didn't you?"

Mr. Bland took the hat from Simon and gave him back a pound and then seemed anxious to be rid of them.

G

" Good-bye and thank you. . . . Yes! Yes! Half-past nine."

Juliet, with a strange feeling of apprehension, turned and waved to Charles who was so busy talking to his host that he did not notice.

" And he never gave us any tea after all," Simon protested as they walked away. " I wonder why he's so keen on our Johnny? You were as good as he was, Juliet."

She squeezed his arm. He was a nice brother.

They bought some tea, and although many people spoke to them they got away as soon as they could. Foxy was no longer at the entrance, which disappointed Simon.

" I hope we can find a village or some cottages," he said. " I'm not looking forward to cycling back here after nine o'clock."

Just after this they caught up a dear old lady and asked her if there was anywhere near where they could eat and sleep the night.

" Well, my dears! Fancy you asking me! I heard you just now in the sunk garden my pretty dear, and very good you were. But haven't you got no homes, and where's the romantic young man with his fiddle? "

" He'll be coming later," Juliet said briefly, and then tried to explain about their holiday and how they were willing to help anyone in the house or garden in exchange for beds and food.

Mrs. Hawkins, for this was her name, beamed on them.

" Come you with me, my dears. But ten minutes' walk and there's Honeysuckle Cottage waiting for you. My daughter is away so you can have her room, my dear, and I dare say the two boys can manage in the parlour somehow or other. . . . And there can be eggs for supper and brown bread and honey. . . . Come you along and keep me company."

Mrs. Hawkins never stopped talking, but she was kind and friendly and her tiny, four-roomed cottage, set back a little from the road, was as bright and shiny as its mistress. Juliet didn't get her bath, but there was plenty of hot water and when they sat down to supper in the kitchen the Buckinghams had almost forgotten Charles until their hostess said:

" That Mr. Bland, now. He spoke very nice before you did your acting. He's a real gentleman but it's a pity he's no wife to share Maryknoll with him. All alone in that big house with only Mr. Simmonds to look after him. . . . And always a playing away on his piano—when he's there, that is."

" Does he go away a lot? " Juliet asked as she cracked her second egg.

" None knows much of what goes on at Maryknoll. That Simmonds keeps hisself to hisself, but 'tis said that Mr. Bland goes a lot to London to concerts and the like, for he's a great musician they say. Once every year, though, Maryknoll is opened for all and as I likes to see the flowers and such I goes along. . . . He's a real gentleman though, and speaks that nicely to one and all."

They had already explained that they were going to fetch Charles at half-past nine, so after they had helped the old lady to wash up and carried down an odd assort-ment of bedding into the parlour, they wandered out into the tiny garden.

" I've enjoyed my day," Juliet said. " What about you, Simon? We've managed all right, haven't we? "

Her brother yawned and nodded.

" It's been a bit tiring, but we have made some money. When are you going to ring up the parents? "

" I will in the morning. . . . Simon. I wish I knew why Mr. Bland wanted us out of the way? "

" Let's go and see. It must be a quarter past nine. We'll go on the bikes."

Maryknoll was very different in the dark and without its crowd of visitors. They put their cycles just inside the iron gates which were now closed, and walked up the drive in the dark. It was so quiet and still that the crunch of their shoes on the gravel seemed doubly loud, but they both stopped in surprise when they turned the corner from which the house should have been visible. All they could see was the bulk of the great cedar and a shadowy shape behind it. No light showed in any window.

" I thought that room with the white piano was in the front," Simon said.

" So it was. I'm sure of it. I expect they're in a room at the back. Let's ring the bell."

They rang three times without an answer. The house remained dark and still.

Simon's teeth began to chatter with a fear he could not explain. Suddenly he hated Maryknoll.

" Stop that silly noise," Juliet said loudly to give herself courage. " Pull yourself together, Simon. It's just that they're out in the garden somewhere or at the back and can't hear the bell. I'm going to ring again," and she kept her finger on the bell push for thirty seconds.

Suddenly the front door opened silently.

" Well? " snapped a voice which they already hated. " What do you want? "

It was the foxy man, Simmonds.

"Good evening," Juliet said. "We've called for our friend, John Brown."

The man stared at them blankly.

"You have made a mistake. This is the house of Mr. Bland. There is nobody here of the name of Brown."

Juliet forced a shaky laugh.

"John Brown is a boy who came with us to the show this afternoon. He played the fiddle and Mr. Bland asked him to stay to supper and play to him after. Mr. Bland knows all about it and told us to come back for him at half-past nine. Of course he's here. He *must* be!"

"You are mistaken. There is no boy here. This is a private house. Please go away," and he closed the door firmly.

As they stared at each other in surprise and fear they heard the bolts slide home.

CHAPTER 5

CHARLES ALONE

" THAT's that, my boy," Mr. Bland had said to Charles as the disconsolate Buckinghams walked away. " No doubt they are very pleasant and amusing children but you and I have something very much more important to discuss. Charming though your young friend, the budding actress, may be, I do not think she has much appreciation of music and it is of music, and this violin in particular, that we must talk. . . . No doubt you would like some tea. Let us see what Simmonds can produce," and he turned into the drawing-room and rang a bell.

Charles, in a moment of sudden panic, ran a few steps down to the lawn. He was too late to see Juliet turn and wave, but just in time to see her gleaming head in the crowd down by the tea-tent. Suddenly he regretted his decision to stay behind. What did the money matter? Already, in a few short and crowded hours, these two seemed the best friends he had ever had. He had never known many girls but Juliet's friendly smile of welcome over her garden wall this morning, had made him forget the miseries of yesterday, and when he thought of how good the Buckinghams had both been about trusting him and not nagging him about his secret he was ashamed of himself. He ought never to have let them go. They were his friends and they'd promised never to desert each other, and just because this man, Bland, had made a fuss of him he had deserted them. Maybe it wasn't too late to catch them now?

But before he could move he felt a hand on his arm and Mr. Bland said:

"Don't go away, my boy. Your friends will look after themselves and will be back at half-past nine for you. Did you not hear them promise? We shall be very pleasantly occupied until then, I assure you."

"I'm sorry, sir, but I'd rather go with them. It doesn't matter about the money. I'll come back presently if you like—after we've found somewhere to camp."

"Nonsense, John—I think you said your name was John Brown, did you not? Come in here in the cool and have some tea and then perhaps you can play again to the assembled company."

Miserably Charles followed his host into the cool drawing-room and perched himself on the edge of a divan, while the other sat on the piano stool and talked to him of music to put him at his ease. Then the door opened to admit Simmonds with a well-loaded tea trolley which he pushed towards his master, and Charles suddenly realized that he was hungry and thirsty. He was not very difficult to flatter a little and when Mr. Bland led him out to the terrace later and announced that, "Our young friend, the musician, has agreed to play for us again," some of the chatter died down and a few people moved up towards him.

He may have been tired, and certainly he missed Juliet and Simon, but somehow this time it was different. The fun and excitement had gone with most of the crowds and there was something about Mr. Bland which made him uneasy and suspicious.

The shadows were lengthening across the lawn and from the tea-tent came the clatter of crockery as he stood before the french windows with his fiddle in his hand feeling unhappy and alone. In the few seconds before he lifted his bow and began to play he thought again of his room at Manlands and wondered what had been happening there. He wondered for the thousandth time what his mother was doing, and then his thoughts went back to Ludlow Castle and the way Juliet had chattered to him as they crossed the courtyard and how Simon had fooled them both by sleeping in the sun while they were working.

"You may start, my boy," came Mr. Bland's soft voice from behind him. "Don't stand there dreaming."

It was not so bad when he began and forgot the silly, pink faces staring up at him, but he knew he was not playing well. He remembered the Rachmaninoff this time and felt strangely moved as he recalled how much better he had played it in the garden at Leasend this morning. He was not quite sure but it seemed that the applause was perfunctory when he lowered his bow after ten minutes and Mr. Bland said, "That will do, my boy. Thank you. Perhaps you will wait just inside the room for me. I shall not be long. Do not go any farther but amuse yourself at the piano if you wish."

For a moment Charles wondered whether there was time for him to escape, and then realized that he did not know where the Buckinghams were and that they would be coming back here for him at half-past nine. This was the only meeting place they had so, rather resignedly, he put the fiddle back in its case and sat down at the piano while Mr. Bland said "Good-bye" to his guests outside the open windows.

Charles felt that his host was losing some of his charm and certainly his farewells were briefer than the greetings he had given to some of the charming ladies earlier in the afternoon. Twice he turned and glanced into the room and then, reassured that Charles was still there, resumed his duties even more briskly than before.

His voice drifted through the open window.

" Good-bye ! Good-bye ! Delighted you could come. . . . A splendid afternoon. . . . Most gratifying. . . . Shall look forward to seeing you next year. . . . Not at all, madam. Not at all. . . . Farewell, dear lady. . . . Yes. Of course. . . . The Committee will announce the amount raised in due course. . . . Good-bye."

The voice and the trite replies droned on. The dusk deepened in the gracious room. Charles yawned. He rested his head on his arms which were crossed on the keyboard and dozed. Then he slept.

When he woke a shaded lamp was glowing on the white piano and Mr. Bland, with the light reflected oddly from his spectacles, was standing a few feet away staring at him.

" I'm sorry, sir," Charles mumbled as he scrambled off the stool, " I must have been very sleepy."

There was a long pause before the man answered. " I think you told me that your name was John Brown."

" I did, sir."

" Where do you live and how did you get here to-day? "

" I told you, sir. I'm on a cycling holiday with my friends, Juliet and Simon."

" Where did you learn to play the violin? Who teaches you? "

Charles blinked, rubbed his eyes and reached for the violin case on the piano. Suddenly he was quite certain that it had been moved. There was no particular reason why he should remember where he had put it when he sat down, but he was sure that it was now at least two feet nearer the window end of the piano top. It had been moved while he slept, and when he looked more carefully he saw that one of the clasps of the lid was undone and he was positive that he would not have been so careless. Of course there was no real reason why Mr. Septimus Bland, the musician, should not examine the violin, but it was odd that he should wish to do so again while its owner was asleep. But why be so secret and underhand about it? And his questions just now had been more than odd—they had been unpleasantly abrupt, with a ring of authority in them which Charles did not like. It was difficult to see him properly now in the half light, but Charles sensed a change in the man—almost a change of appearance. There was a suggestion in the way he was standing as well as in the tone of his voice that the benevolent, charming and cultured host of the afternoon had another side of his personality.

Charles felt his heart begin to thump uncomfortably, and then his wits came back.

"Where do I learn the violin, sir? I have lessons at home. I'm very keen. . . . I say, sir. I'm afraid I was very rude just now dropping off to sleep like that and I'm most disgustingly dirty. It's really most kind of you to ask me to stay for a meal, but I'm only in these old holiday clothes and I must have been making your piano stool dirty," and he turned and began to brush the tapestry industriously with his hand.

Mr. Bland moved out of the centre of light cast by the little lamp and his feet made no sound on the soft carpet.

"Don't act like a fool, my boy. Stop that fidgeting."

" I'm sorry," Charles straightened and tried his most charming smile. " I was only feeling rather ashamed of myself. Could I have a wash, please, and a clothes brush? "

Mr. Bland moved to the door, switched on some hidden lights and pressed a bell push. The man, Simmonds, might have been waiting outside so quickly did he answer the summons.

" Ah! Simmonds. Thank you. Our young friend here needs some attention. A hairbrush seems indicated and certainly a clothes brush. Soap and water, too. Will you look after him? "

The man in black stood aside and directed the briefest glance from his pale eyes to Charles.

" Go with Simmonds, my boy. He will show you the way and I shall be awaiting your return eagerly. . . . There is no need for you to take the violin with you. It will be quite safe here."

But Charles pretended not to hear the last remark and the case was under his arm as he followed Simmonds into the hall and down a corridor to a tiled cloakroom at the end.

" You will find everything you require," the man-servant said briefly, and shut the door.

Charles was beginning to wonder whether his decision not to try an escape was wise, for Mr. Bland's questions were awkward and insistent and might very well become more pressing. There was no doubt, either, that the violin had been examined while he was asleep and his host's curiosity about this was particularly worrying. As he washed and tidied himself he glanced at the window above the wash basin. It was small and opened from the bottom outwards, and even if smashed and forced from the frame he was fairly certain that he was too big to squeeze through. For a moment he considered pushing the violin out in the hope of finding it later, but soon dismissed this idea. He dared not run such a risk but he was certainly not looking forward to the next hour. He suspected now that he was alone in the house with Mr. Bland and Simmonds, and the prospect was not very pleasant. If only the others had been with him it would have been an easy situation to manage, but Mr. Bland had a persuasive manner and an enticing tongue and Charles was certain that he was not nearly so jolly and easy-going as he had first looked. He wished that he knew the reason behind his curiosity, too.

Charles rather absent-mindedly combed his hair, then picked up the violin case and, very quietly, opened the door. Simmonds was leaning against the wall of the corridor waiting for him, and without a word, led him back to a smaller room where Mr. Bland was sitting beside a sweet-smelling log fire sipping a glass of sherry.

" This is my study, John. I am not at all sure what boys of your age drink before a civilized dinner, but I doubt if it is sherry. Is it, perhaps, what is known as ' ginger-pop '? "

He shivered elegantly while Charles winced.

" No thank you, sir. I won't have anything now."

" I see you took your instrument with you, John. You must be very attached to it."

Charles flushed. " Yes, sir. I am."

" I have some very interesting books on music in this room. If you are as intelligent as I think you are you might like to borrow some. You will be welcome at any time. . . . Do you live far away, John? Too far to cycle over sometimes and play to me? I hope not."

Charles mumbled something, well aware that Mr. Bland was watching him carefully and was thankful that before being faced with a coherent reply Simmonds opened the door and announced dinner.

Manlands was a beautiful and well equipped house and Charles had been brought up to appreciate it, but Maryknoll was decorated and furnished with an exquisite taste that was new to him. A schoolboy can hardly be a judge of antique furniture, glass and silver, but Charles had an instinctive sympathy for anything beautiful and he was nearly rude enough to gasp and express his pleasure when he walked into the dining-room.

White, wax candles burned with unwavering flames on the mahogany table in the centre of which was a crystal bowl of roses. Three gleaming glasses by his place did not daunt Charles and he sat down without a glance at Simmonds who pulled out his chair for him.

Mr. Bland obviously enjoyed his food and this dinner was very good—melon, lamb chops with fresh peas and fruit with ice-cream. As soon as he started to eat he became more friendly. He put Charles at his ease by talking of music and was clever enough never to patronize him, so it was not long before the boy forgot his suspicions of half an hour ago. Mr. Bland had a good memory, too, and offered some friendly and critical comment on the music which Charles had played in the sunk garden.

"That little Mozart piece is quite fascinating, John, but I suspect it is beyond your powers. If you have finished your ice we will go back to the music room and perhaps you will play it to me again? It is very ambitious and I am surprised that your professor permits you to attempt it. . . . Oh, Simmonds! Our guest left his violin in my study. Perhaps you will fetch it for us. Thank you!"

As he walked out into the hall behind his host Charles thought he detected a sneer on the manservant's face and realized that he had rather made a fool of himself by taking his fiddle to the cloakroom and then leaving it unguarded in the study, and his face was red with embarrassment when the man handed it to him a few minutes later.

"Better examine it carefully," Mr. Bland smiled. "Somebody might have tampered with it. . . . Do you mind if I try it myself? I can see that it is a very sympathetic instrument."

Charles' suspicions flickered up for a moment, but it was difficult to refuse such a natural and courteous request so he passed it over. Mr. Bland waited while Simmonds put the coffee tray on a stool, drew the curtains and closed the door softly behind him, then he stood up, leaned against the white piano and drew the bow lovingly across the strings. There was no doubt that he was a musician, but after playing for only a few minutes he put down the bow and took the violin over to the standard lamp in the corner. Then he turned to Charles and said:

"I want you to tell me truthfully, my boy, where did you get this violin?" and there was a hard ring to his voice that sent a little shiver of apprehension down Charles' spine.

"I don't want to be rude, sir, but I cannot see why I should answer you. It is nothing to do with you but I promise you that it is mine. Please may I have it back?"

Mr. Bland swung the violin gently to and fro from his fingers.

" I want you to tell me truthfully, my boy, where did you get this violin? "

" I am not at all sure that it does belong to you. It is not the sort of instrument that a schoolboy would possess. Can you prove that it is yours? I tell you frankly my boy, that my suspicions are aroused."

Charles flushed at the insult of the last words.

" I can only give you my word of honour. It is mine. My father gave it to me."

The man smiled faintly.

" I think that is a lie. There is a signature scratched on the side of the violin in my hand and it is certainly not that of a gentleman named Brown."

Too late Charles realized that he had been trapped. He would have to tell the truth now.

" The signature is my father's. My name is not Brown.

It is Charles Renislau and my father was Alex Renislau who died in the defence of Warsaw. I said my name was Brown because— "

" Because what? Why do you wish to hide the fact that you are the son of a great composer? . . . I notice that you are trying to think of an answer. . . . No, no, Master Brown. To say that you are the son of Alex Renislau just because you have a violin which bears his signature—or possibly a forged signature—is easy enough, but how do I know that you have not stolen this fiddle, particularly as you are wandering about the country with two other rascally children masquerading under false names? "

" That's not true, sir. Juliet and Simon are my friends and those are their real names. But I am Charles Renislau, whatever you say."

" Then why do you call yourself Brown? "

" I'd rather not tell you and I don't suppose you'd believe me if I did. . . . Please give me back my father's fiddle and let me go."

Mr. Bland crossed the room and sat on the piano stool, but he still kept the violin in his hands.

" You're story is so absurd that it may be true. Listen, boy. I would like to buy this violin from you. I will give you twenty pounds for it."

" I'm sorry, sir, but I wouldn't sell it for any money in the world. It was my father's and I will never part with it."

" Think carefully. You could do a great deal with twenty pounds."

Charles shook his head. " No, sir. Not for any price. You don't seem to understand what I've just told you. Please give it to me now and let me go and meet my friends. It's nearly nine o'clock and they'll be on their way, I expect."

Mr. Bland glanced at the clock and his voice hardened.

" You are hiding something, Brown—if that is your name, which I doubt as much as the fantastic suggestion that it is Renislau. I am certain of it. I believe this violin to be stolen and I am going to inform the police of your presence here. What do you say to that? "

Charles thought quickly. It looked as if he would soon be home with his tail between his legs as Hetty had warned him. This was a poor sort of end to the adventure and his high hopes of proving his independence. And how Cyril and Derek would smirk and sneer! He would have to tell the police his address and they would not waste much time in checking it. But even being sent home mattered nothing so long as he could get the violin back safely.

" Very well, sir," he said firmly. " You can go to the police if you wish. I'm not afraid. I don't mind giving them my address, but I don't intend to give it to you. . . . Please let me go now. You've no right to keep me here and no right to my violin."

This outburst apparently impressed the other for he stared at Charles for a long time without speaking. Then he raised the violin to his chin again and, to the boy's amazement played, very haltingly, a plaintive theme which was only too familiar to him.

" Do you know that air, my boy? "

" Yes, I do. You haven't got it quite right but it is the motif of my father's last Violin Concerto. He finished it in 1938 my mother says, and although it has been performed abroad it has not yet been played in England. My mother taught it to me."

H

Bland put down the violin and looked at him.

" I see. Perhaps you are right. Where is your mother? "

" In Switzerland. I think she's been ill."

" Would money help her to get better? I will give a lot of money for the Renislau fiddle. More than twenty pounds. Much more. Enough to buy a motor cycle and to make your mother well." . . .

Bland was showing some emotion. The words came quickly and eagerly as he leaned forward and put his hand on the boy's knee. But poor Charles was tired, bewildered and scared. The situation seemed completely unreal and the other's personality was so strong that he began to fear that he might soon give way.

" Let me go now, sir," he pleaded. " I promise I'll come back in the morning and tell you whether I really will sell it. Perhaps the money would be more important after all, but I must think it over. Surely you see that I can't decide a thing like this right away? "

Mr. Bland looked up at the clock the hands of which showed ten past nine. Then he passed Charles the violin and said, " But you'd never come back. I know you wouldn't. . . . But all the same I would like you to think this over and decide as quickly as you can. . . . Come with me." . . .

He crossed the room and pressed the bell push and while waiting he stood and stared at Charles as if considering an important problem in which the boy was involved. When Simmonds came he said, " Come with us, Simmonds, please, just to make sure that our young friend behaves himself. He has decided to spend the night with us. . . . The little room overlooking the yard is too high for a foolhardy leap from the window and would do very well I think. . . . Now then, my boy.

I will lead the way and Simmonds will follow you closely.
. . . And take the violin, of course, but remember that
you will probably be very pleased to sell it to me in
the morning."

There was no escape. Foxy Simmonds was at his elbow
and Mr. Bland only a pace ahead. Charles knew he had
not one chance in a million of getting away so, sick at
heart and feeling that he had failed completely, but with
his violin case under his arm, he followed the master
of Maryknoll up the beautifully proportioned staircase.

" I hope you will sleep well," Mr. Bland said as he
opened the door of a small bedroom. " I am afraid you
will have to manage without your personal luggage for
neither of us can go and hunt for it now, and I think it
would be better if you removed the electric light bulb,
Simmonds. When the friends of our friend arrive here
shortly it would never do for them to see a light in
this bedroom. . . . Sleep as well as you can, Brown or
Renislau, and remember that in the morning we will
talk again and I am quite certain that you will be glad
to sell me the violin. . . . Good night to you."

Simmonds grinned at him viciously as they went out
and locked the door behind them, while Charles sat on
the edge of the bed in the darkness and rested his head
in his hands.

CHAPTER 6

THE RESCUE

IT was not long after Charles had been locked in the bedroom on the first floor of Maryknoll that Juliet and Simon were locked out. For a long minute they stood on the step after Simmonds had closed the door in their faces, without even speaking—Simon shaking with one of his very rare tempers, while his sister was suddenly afraid. It was only a few hours ago that this lovely house and garden were alive with happy people. Only a few hours ago that she had been so proud that she had been able to stand up before a crowd of strangers and do well enough not to shame her brother and her new friend. Now, with the darkness, everything had changed. The house seemed lifeless and deserted.

Simon spoke first.

" Let's get out of here. . . . Come on Julie. . . I hate this place. Something has happened to it. Let's go somewhere where they can't see us and where we can think and talk. . . . I believe that man is watching us."

Rather unexpectedly he felt for her hand. It was cold but her fingers closed reassuringly round his and suddenly he felt a warm rush of affection for the sister he always took for granted.

" Come on, Julie! No use standing here."

Without a word she turned and they walked together down the drive, past the entrance to the field where they had left their bicycles earlier in the afternoon, through the iron gates and into the lane, and not until then

did Juliet say, " I don't believe him, Simon. He's a liar.
Something has happened and they're playing a trick on
us. What shall we do? "

He realized then that she was still holding his hand
so tightly that all feeling had gone from his fingers.
He pulled them free and rubbed them as he said:

" I don't know. Let's think carefully. I'm sure it's
no good going back and ringing the bell again. He bolted
the door and it's not likely that they'd answer a second
time."

" But he pretended he'd never seen us or Johnny,"
Juliet whispered. " That's what was so horrible! He
just pretended that there wasn't any such person. He
didn't deny that Mr. Bland lived there but tried to make
us feel that there isn't any Johnny Brown at all."

" There isn't! " Simon smiled in the dark. " We know
that's not his name."

" But *why?* " his sister protested. " *Why* are they pretending that? Has Johnny gone off on his own do you
think? But if he had, surely that man would have
said so? "

" I think he's still in the house," Simon said shrewdly.
" There's something very peculiar about Mr. Bland, but
I can't think what it is. I don't know *why* they want us
to go away, but I'm sure that they do and that's a
jolly good reason for going back. Will you come? "

" Of course. Don't let's do anything until we're as
certain as we can be that Johnny isn't there. We did
promise to stick to each other and if he has gone off
on his own I'm sure that somehow or other he'd leave
us a message."

" Where? " Simon asked. " That's the point. He
doesn't know where we've been. All that he could be

sure of was that we would come back here at half-past nine."

"I know, and it's because of that I believe he's in the house and maybe a prisoner, although I can't think why. Surely they wouldn't lock him up and make him play to them, Simon? Why should they keep him there? "

"We don't really know anything about him, Julie. . . . I mean I'm quite sure he's a decent chap and all that, but we do know he's run away from home and he is rather a mystery."

"We promised to trust him. I do trust him, although I think that he ought to have come with us, but I do wish I knew why Mr. Bland was so interested in him. I don't think it's just because he plays the fiddle so well. . . . Let's creep back through the bushes and then go all round the outside of the house. I was scared before but I shan't mind now."

"Don't close the gates this time," Simon whispered. "We may want to get out in a hurry! . . . And we mustn't go on the lawn or anywhere in the open 'cos they may be watching for us, though I don't see why they should! "

The moon was just coming up but it was very dark under the trees as they made their way back towards the house. Simon need not have worried too much about being seen on the lawn for when they reached the edge of the trees they realized that the gardens were still littered with chairs, trestles and benches.

"I didn't notice that they hadn't cleared up when we came up the drive," Juliet whispered. "I don't think we should be seen if we dodged or crawled across the lawn, which we shall have to do if we want to explore all round the house."

Simon nodded in the dark.

"Stay here for a bit. Let's just watch and see if a light pops up anywhere. I shouldn't think that even the delightful Mr. Simmonds goes to bed in the dark."

They crouched in the undergrowth while the moon slid up the spangled sky and threw grotesque shadows across the lawns of Maryknoll. There was no sign nor sound of life from the big house. No breath of wind stirred the tree tops and it was almost a relief to the two watchers when a great white owl drifted by soundlessly over their heads.

Juliet fidgeted and began to rub her leg.

"I must move, Simon. My foot has gone to sleep. Let's go on now. There's nothing to see here. . . . Just wait till I've dodged across to the tea-tent behind these chairs and then follow me."

Simon watched her as she squirmed across the grass and almost called a warning when she looked up and the moonlight gleamed on her blonde head. As soon as she waved to him from the shadow of the marquee he followed her as quietly as possible.

"No lights this side either," Simon whispered. "Surely they don't all go to bed before ten? I don't like this place, Juliet. It gives me the creeps. It's so quiet."

"I'm not going back to Mrs. Hawkins until we've been right round the house," Juliet said. "Let's get on."

This time they had not moved very far when Simon drew in his breath sharply and grabbed his sister's arm. They stood stock still and then he put his lips to her ear and breathed, "I heard something. I'm sure it was a voice. . . . Listen."

They strained their ears in vain and then Juliet whispered, "I can't hear anything but I'm not sure that

I didn't see a gleam of light down at the far corner—
it would be at the window of the last room on the
left on the ground level. . . . Can you see anything? "

He shook his head. " Let's get nearer. There's a rose
bed or something close to that window."

When they were near enough, and looking at the
window from a different angle, Simon said, " You're
right, Julie. There is a light there. I bet the window
is open behind the curtains and what I heard just now
was somebody talking inside the room. . . . Let's try
and look in."

They moved from the shelter of the rose trees and
crept as quietly as they could across a gravel path. This
side of the house was in dense shadow and Juliet, in
front, moved step by step with her hands stretched before her. A stone moved under her sandal and rattled
sharply, and while their hearts banged in excitement
they heard again the murmur of a voice from inside the
room.

Simon shivered as he thought, " There's no answer.
It's someone talking to himself! "

Another few paces and they reached the stone step
outside a narrow french window, one side of which was
open. A heavy curtain prevented them from seeing inside
so Simon crouched down on his knees and very gently
moved it with his fingers. Then he tugged Juliet's shorts
and signalled that she should stand above him and make
a gap for herself higher up.

They saw a comfortable, book-lined room containing
a desk and three big, leather easy-chairs. In one of the
latter, near the remains of a log fire, Mr. Bland was
lounging with his back to the window. There was a
cigar in his right hand and a telephone in his left.

" . . . A most remarkable stroke of luck," they heard him say. " Most remarkable, and I have no doubt at all that it is genuine. . . . I have not time to tell you the whole story now but I do assure you that the name is on it and by an astonishing coincidence the son has brought it to me. . . . What did you say? . . . Yes. His son. . . . Oh, yes. There was a son. We knew that. And a wife, too, who brought the boy to England at the time, but nobody knew what happened to them. . . . But never mind about that now. The point is that I have what matters. . . . Now listen, for this is where you come in. Rankin. . . . Yes. Yes. Hiram Rankin, of course. Rankin has been over here for some weeks but I suspect he will be sailing for New York in the *Queen Mary* at the week-end. Check this up. . . . No! He will not be flying. He hates it. . . . I beg your pardon? You know all about him? . . . Splendid, my dear fellow. Splendid! . . . He is staying for the Albert Hall this week, you say! Excellent . . . He must be contacted at once and told what we have for him. He will find it difficult to believe but I assure you that it is so. . . . It will be very expensive but he will pay. . . . I will bring it south to-morrow. . . . Yes. Yes! Chelsea, of course. . . . Get into touch with me there sometime in the evening. . . ." and just then he flicked the ash of his cigar into the hearth and then stood up and faced the window with the telephone in his hand.

Juliet felt the strength go out of her knees and only just prevented herself from clutching at the curtain. At her feet Simon was wriggling away from the window, and almost before she realized what was happening they were both running desperately across the grass to the shelter of some bushes.

" The old devil," Simon gasped. " Did you see his face when he turned round, Julie? That was awful? Do you think he saw us? "

" Lie flat behind this bush," she whispered. " He can't see us but we shall be able to spot him if he looks out with the light behind him. . . . Your teeth are chattering again, Simon. Do stop it."

" I'm only excited. I bet a bloodhound's teeth chatter when he's on the trail."

They lay, side by side, on the dry leaves with their eyes fixed on the window at the corner of the house. After a little Juliet whispered, " I was just thinking about what we heard just now. It doesn't make sense to me and it doesn't help us to find Johnny. That's what we've come here for, isn't it? "

" There's something I wanted to tell you," Simon said irrelevantly. " If we're going to do much of this sort of thing you must cover up that hair of yours. . . . You waved it about in the moonlight when you were crossing the lawn just now and I'm sure you'd have been spotted if any one had been looking out."

" I didn't wave it about! What a stupid thing to say. . . . But you're right all the same, Simon. I ought to have worn a scarf—Ssh! Look! "

Suddenly one of the curtains of Mr. Bland's study was pulled aside and the master of Maryknoll stood for a moment on the step, outlined in the orange light behind him. They saw the end of his cigar glow as he raised it to his lips and then he stepped out into the garden and they heard his shoes scrunch on the gravel.

Poor Juliet, suddenly conscious of her gleaming hair, crouched even lower under the bushes and pulled her brother's dark-sleeved arm across her head.   But

Mr. Bland was obviously in a contemplative mood. He was enjoying his cigar and the peace of the summer night, and as he strolled across his lawn and round his lovely roses he whistled softly to himself. For ten minutes he strolled and whistled until the hidden listeners realized that one little, haunting tune or theme, which was new to them, predominated. Time and time again Mr. Bland whistled or hummed this lovely little air, and then flicked his cigar end away so that it fell not far from the Buckinghams in a shower of sparks, and went back into his study, closing the windows behind him.

"Take your arm off my head, you silly ass," Juliet mumbled. "I'm nearly stifled. . . . Phew! What do we do now? . . . Simon! What do you think he meant on the telephone when he said; "The son has brought it to me?" He must mean Johnny, mustn't he? I wonder who Johnny really is."

Simon rolled over on his back and stretched.

"I've wondered from the very beginning. We'd better try and find out as quickly as possible. If he's still in the house he ought to be able to make some sort of signal."

There were no further signs from the study window and no lights showing anywhere else, so they made their way towards the back of the house through a gate in a hedge. Here they found themselves in a stone-paved yard where there was not much cover. Beyond the entrance to what was obviously the kitchen quarters was another dark mass of shrubbery. They stood just inside the little gate for several minutes listening and peering up at the dark windows above them.

"If only we had a torch," Simon whispered.

"I wouldn't dare use it," Juliet replied. "I've got the feeling all the time that anyone looking out can see us more easily than we can see them. The moon will be higher in an hour and that might help, but I'm not sure how long we dare wait here. I should think old Mrs. Hawkins will be wondering where we are. I told her that we'd be back with Johnny by ten."

"I'd forgotten about her. What do you think she'll do? We must have been here nearly an hour."

Then, without any warning, they heard the unmistakable sound of a window being opened somewhere above their heads. Juliet pushed open the gate behind her and pulled her brother back into the shadow of the hedge.

"Where was that, Simon? I didn't see a light. Somebody is looking out of a dark room."

Simon's teeth were chattering again and it was a minute before he answered, "I'm not liking this very much. I hope I'm not scared, but I think I am!"

Juliet was not feeling particularly brave herself and did not quite know what to do next, but before she could answer they had another surprise. Quite clearly, through the stillness of the night, came the sound of somebody whistling — and what was even more extraordinary, the hidden watcher was whistling the same odd little air that Mr. Bland had been whistling when he was strolling in his garden only a few minutes ago.

"It's old Bland," Simon whispered. "It's the old boy himself. He's gone to bed."

But in the dark shadow of the hedge Juliet was frowning. She had been brought up to appreciate music and had a very good ear. There was somehow something different about this latest performance. The tune was certainly the same but not the whistler.

" I don't believe it is Bland," she whispered. " It sounds different to me. It's softer."

She was still searching for the words to describe her muddled impressions when the whistling stopped.

" It was the same to me," Simon said. " Just a silly little tune. Of course it's Bland. Who else could it be? "

" It might be Johnny, you idiot. I'm going back there. Will you come too? Let's keep flat up against the wall of the house and risk it. If anyone is looking out they're not so likely to see us. If they do and if it is Bland or that foxy Simmonds and they give the alarm, we shall have to run for it. Are you game? "

" I suppose so, Julie. I'm having a terrible experience but I suppose I'd better go through with it. I'm beginning to wish we'd never met John Brown."

Juliet smiled in the darkness and took hold of his sleeve. " You're not, you know. Come on! "

They crept through the gate again and, keeping in the shadow, flattened themselves against the wall of the house and listened. All was quiet. It was difficult to look up at the windows on the upper floors, but as Simon was confident that the window which they had heard being opened was at the far end they advanced cautiously, step by step, and strained their ears for any fresh sound. They had some awkward moments passing the back door and had not many more yards to go before reaching the shrubbery by the corner of the house when Juliet, who was in front, kicked against an empty tin. The noise seemed deafening and she only choked back a sob of disappointment with difficulty. Close against her she could feel her brother trembling with excitement or fear, and then the whistle came again from almost over their heads. This time Juliet was sure that it was not Mr. Bland

and very softly and sweetly she picked up the tune and whistled a few bars in return. The silence which followed seemed very long, but it was only a few seconds before there came a whispered voice from above. " Who is that? Who's there? "

Juliet clapped her hand over Simon's mouth and whistled the tune again.

" Is that you, Juliet? And Simon? This is—John."

She turned round and facing the wall put her hands over her mouth and whispered so that the sound travelled upwards.

" Yes, Johnny. We're here. What's happened? "

She flushed in the darkness when she heard his sigh of relief and whispered words, " You're marvellous, Juliet. I knew you'd come. What did they say to you? "

" Slammed the door in our faces, Johnny, and said you weren't here. We didn't believe them and here we are. Do you want to be rescued? Are you all right? What have they done to you? "

" I'm locked in and I don't know what they're going to do. That man, Bland, wants my fiddle. Can you get me out? "

" When you two have finished your private conversation," Simon whispered peevishly, " p'raps you'd remember that I'm here too. Of course we can get you out, John. That's what we've come for, and anyway I've spent too long round this place. I want to get back to the nice Mrs. Hawkins and go to bed."

Charles chuckled.

" If you could find a rope or a ladder it wouldn't take long. They've taken the light away and there are no sheets or blankets on the bed. There's nothing I can make a rope with. . . . I say, Juliet? "

" What is it? I'm still here."

" Don't be too long, will you. I'm afraid that man, Simmonds, will come back and I don't want him to catch you."

Simon snorted his disgust.

" Push some furniture in front of the door so that they can't get in and we'll go and find a ladder or a rope. We'll be as quiet and quick as we can and I expect we'll hear if they come banging on your door."

" Keep a look out of the window while we're gone," Juliet whispered. " Bland has been strolling about outside. If you see anyone who isn't us whistle that tune again as loudly as you can as a warning and we'll keep out of the way."

" You'd better put that tin you fell over in the middle of the path," Simon advised. " That makes a wonderful warning. Come on! Let's find the gardener's sheds."

When they reached the shrubbery Juliet turned and waved to the darker shadow that was the prisoner's open window, and perhaps it was as well that her brother did not see her.

Simon, in spite of his recent remarks about bed, was now behaving like a small, excited terrier. If he had possessed a tail he would have been wagging it as he hunted the strange country bordering the kitchen garden. He dragged Juliet along paths between thick hedges, stumbled over rubbish heaps, skirted a row of glass frames, galloped by a greenhouse and stopped triumphantly before a long, wooden potting shed.

" I bet we find something here," he gasped, " and if the door is locked we'll bash it in. . . . I want to get this over and—"

" I know, darling. You want to get it over and go

back to Mrs. Hawkins and go to bed. Of course you do.
You must be a very tired little boy. You won't have to
do any bashing, anyway, 'cos it is open. All we want
now is a light."

" If we could find John's bike we could borrow the
lamp, but it will take too long to find. I should think
we're completely lost now, anyway. . . . Let's go and
grope."

They had to do a lot of groping but the moon was
higher now and a little light found its way through the
grimy windows of the shed. There seemed everything
there but rope—flower pots, old boxes, tools, a sack of
potatoes, some nasty looking, twisty, dry roots and, much
to Juliet's terror, a rat. Simon, who was now quite reck-
less, saw the latter just when it was scuttling for shelter
and flung a handful of potatoes at it. Then he went on
searching without noticing that his sister had run outside.

" Sorry, Simon," she whispered from the door, " but
I can't stand them. I've gone cold down the back and
if I come in again I shall scream."

" There's no rope in here," he replied. " I'm sure there
isn't. I can't think why they don't have rope in a garden of this size. . . . Do you think there's another shed
somewhere, Julie? Will you go and explore and I'll stay
here and fight the rats? "

She didn't like the idea of this suggestion very much
but had only moved a few steps when Simon ran to
the door.

" All right. Come back. I've found something. It's
not rope but I think it will do."

What he had discovered was a pile of netting such
as is used for stretching over strawberry beds to keep
the birds away.

" If we twist it up into a sort of rope it should bear his weight," Juliet agreed. " Let's go and try. I want to get out of this place, too."

Charles was leaning from the window waiting for them and they were not very pleased with his greeting —" I thought you were never coming."

" There's no rope and no ladder," Simon said tersely, " but we're going to throw you up a bundle of netting. Catch it and then twist it up and tie the end to something up there and come down as quickly as you can."

Charles caught the bundle at the third attempt and ten minutes later whispered that he was ready. First, he lowered the violin case, which Juliet had to reach up to catch, and then followed himself. The twisted rope of netting was not very long and he had to drop the last six feet. Almost before he had got off his knees Simon was jumping for the end of the rope.

" Let's pull it down if we can and put it back in the shed. I'd like to keep them guessing about your escape in the morning."

The combined weight of the three of them was enough to loosen the knot which Charles had made round the leg of the bed, and the netting fell over their heads as they tumbled to the ground together.

" Now throw this in the shed again and let's run for it," Juliet gasped. " Keep in the shadows."

Five minutes later all three, with their bicycles, were outside the closed gates of Maryknoll. None of them had had much to say until they were safe in the lane and then, to the Buckinghams' surprise and embarrassment, Charles dropped his bicycle on the green verge and came towards them with outstretched hands. Simon dashed away in alarm but Juliet stood her ground.

I

" . . . let's run for it," Juliet gasped. " Keep in the shadows."

" How can I thank you, my new and wonderful friends? If was you, Juliet, who said first that the three of us should stick together, and in a few hours you have proved what loyalty really means. . . . How can I ever show you my gratitude? " and then suddenly, and for the first time in her life, Juliet found her hand being kissed. She grabbed it away and glimpsed her brother's horror-stricken face in the moonlight, jumped on her bicycle and pedalled away as fast as she could.

They reached Honeysuckle Cottage without further incident and Charles was introduced to the garrulous Mrs. Hawkins, who did not seem very curious about their late arrival, although they were surprised to see that it was only eleven o'clock.

" What you've been up to is no business of mine after all," she said, " and I'm off to my bed now and very welcome it will be. Flower Shows and the like are all very well in their places, but they're that hard on the feet I find. . . . You two boys have got to manage as best you can in the parlour—one could sleep on the sofy, I reckon, and t'other on the hearthrug and the feather bed I've brought down. . . . You know where you are, my dear, and if you would like a cup of cocoa afore you all go off the milk is ready in the saucepan on the stove right behind you. . . . So now I'll be saying ' Good-night '—and ' God bless you all,' " she added unexpectedly, " and I'm right glad to have a bit of young life round the place again."

She looked a little surprised as Charles got up and opened the door for her and then swept out with an odd little curtsey to them all.

" She's a pet," Juliet said, " a darling, a wonderful old pet. . . . I'm so tired that I can hardly keep my eyes open, but before we go to bed you must tell us what happened to you, Johnny. . . . I'll make the cocoa and if we drink that and you talk it ought to keep us awake."

" He'd have told you before if you hadn't dashed off on your bike like that," Simon said wickedly.

They settled down round the kitchen table with their hands round thick mugs of cocoa, but Simon was already nodding when Charles said, " I want to tell you both exactly what happened to-night and I want to tell you who I am and why I ran away. . . . You've both been marvellous to me, and I don't see any sense in pretending I'm John Brown any longer, anyway."

" I expect I'll always call you Johnny now," Juliet smiled, " but it would be nice to know who we're having a holiday with—if you can call it a holiday."

So, with very few interruptions, Charles told them his real name, the true story of his father's violin, of his mother and his life at Manlands.

"I told you that my uncle may tell the police, but I'm not really sure. The trouble now is that Mr. Bland knows who I am and wants to buy my father's violin. . . . I don't know what he intended to do in the morning but he said I should probably have changed my mind by then. I suppose it will be quite easy for him to find out where I live and I'm wondering what will happen if he gets in touch with my uncle."

"The truth is," Simon said, smothering a yawn, "that they locked you up and kept you a prisoner, and then told lies to us. I think there's a mystery about Mr. Bland and I reckon he wants to steal your father's violin, although I can't quite see why. . . . I'm too sleepy to tell you what we heard him saying on the telephone before we found you, but I expect Juliet would. . . . I'm going to bed now, if you can call it bed, and as I'm a bit smaller than you I suppose I shall have to sleep on that slippery sofa. . . . Good-night both. Don't let's get up early. I couldn't bear it."

Juliet then explained to Charles how they had seen the light from Mr. Bland's study and overheard half a conversation on the telephone.

"It wasn't very easy to see him, Johnny—Charles, I mean—and when he did turn round and face the window we lost our nerve and ran for it. So far as I remember he spoke about someone called Rankin who would buy something that he had got, and he said something about the *Queen Mary*, and the Albert Hall, too. Do you know what he meant?"

Charles shook his head.

" Not really, but I'm as sleepy as Simon now. But there is something I want to ask you, Juliet. Who do you think Mr. Bland really is and what is he trying to do? "

" Simon is right I'm sure. He's trying to steal your violin. I don't know who he is any more than you do, except that old Mrs. Hawkins says he keeps ' hisself to hisself,' and that nobody lives at Maryknoll except him and Foxy Simmonds. I can't really believe that, unless Simmonds does all the cooking, but I think she thought they were both a bit peculiar. She said Mr. Bland often goes to London to concerts. I suppose he really is musical? "

" I think so. He must be. He tried the fiddle and he's got that marvellous piano and he talked a lot to me about music—much that I couldn't understand."

He pushed his empty mug into the middle of the table and ran his fingers through his hair. " There's another very peculiar thing though, Juliet. He knows the theme of my father's Violin Concerto and I thought that only Mother and I knew that, because it's never been played in this country."

" I s'pose you don't know whether it's been played abroad or broadcast? "

" I think it has, but the fact that he knew I should recognize it proves that he does believe that I'm Charles Renislau."

Juliet got up, stretched and yawned.

" It's nice to know you properly at last, Charles. The real you, I mean. I'm very proud of my father and his books, so I can understand a little how proud you must be of yours and of the violin. . . . It's been fun to-day,

Charles. I've loved it. Specially the last few hours. . . .
By the way, do you think that Bland may tell the police
that he thinks you've got a stolen violin when he realizes
that you've escaped? "

"Not if he really intends to steal it," Charles said.
"I've an idea that he'll do everything he can to find
us in the morning—or to find me, anyway."

"He won't find you without us, and he won't be
able to bribe you again to leave us, will he? Did he
pay you that pound, by the way? . . . No? I didn't
think he would. . . . Good-night, Johnny—Charles. I'm
going to wash in the sink before I go to bed. There
doesn't seem to be anywhere else to wash here, and of
course my brat of a brother went to bed dirty."

"Thank you again," Charles began, but Juliet pushed
him out of the room. He really was rather emotional
and excitable sometimes!

*   *   *   *

When Simon woke on the shiny horsehair sofa next
morning the sun was streaming into Mrs. Hawkins'
parlour and the grandfather clock in the kitchen was
striking nine. He was extremely stiff and had a slight
headache, which was not surprising as it is doubtful if
the window had been opened for twenty years.

Charles, whom he did not even remember coming to
bed, had already got up for his bedclothes had been
more or less folded and placed in an untidy bundle on
a chair.

Simon sat up and saw a folded piece of paper on the
table beside him. It was addressed to "Juliet and Simon,"
so he opened it.

"*My dear friends,*" he read. "*I have decided to go*

on ahead by myself because I may get you both into trouble if you stick to me. I'm taking the fiddle, of course, and my bike, and think I'll make my way towards London. If you really want to go on helping me maybe you could think of something to keep Bland out of my way or from following me. Please don't think I'm running away or that I don't want you, but I don't want to mess up your holiday. If you would like to see me again and if you think you've put Bland off the track I'll try to be in the porch of Hereford Cathedral between seven and eight to-night. If I'm not there or if you can't manage it, let's try to-morrow morning at nine. Good luck to you both,

Charles."

Simon jumped off the sofa, gave a hitch to his sagging pyjamas and dashed out of the room.

" Hi, Juliet ! " he yelled up the narrow staircase. " Buck up and come down. We've got a job to do for Charlie-boy."

CHAPTER 7

COME TO THE FAIR

AT Simon's second, worried yell for his sister Mrs. Hawkins opened the kitchen door.

" Let the poor lass alone," she scolded. " I looked in on her just now and she'll sleep for hours."

" What room is she in? " Simon demanded. " I'm sorry to make such a row but it's vital that I see her at once," and he started up the narrow stairs.

" There's only two rooms," the old lady began, and then shrugged in despair at the thump and crash of an opening door upstairs. " I don't know what the world is coming to," she murmured without much originality. " These youngsters would never have behaved like this in my days—a'bangin' and shoutin' about in each other's bedrooms."

Another yell came down the staircase.

" It's all right thanks, Mrs. Hawkins. She's awake now. We shan't be long but there'll only be two of us for breakfast."

" That I will *not* believe," she said as she went back to her kitchen and closed the door. " I don't believe that one of them has stopped eating and there were certainly three of them came in last night."

Meanwhile Juliet, in blue striped pyjamas, was sitting up in bed re-reading Charles' note, while her brother prowled up and down the tiny area of floor space between the bed and the window.

" This is the most astounding bedroom I've ever been

in," he was saying. " And look at that bed! You're all
sunk in it! It looks disgusting to me. . . . What do you
think of your precious Charles now? "

" He's not mine," Juliet said indignantly, " and anyway I admire him very much. Can't you see that he's
giving us an opportunity to back out of the adventure
if we want to do so? "

" He knows perfectly well that we don't want to back
out! " her brother protested. " He's known that ever
since we rescued him. I think that every now and then
he does this crazy sort of thing suddenly."

She hugged her knees and flicked back her hair.

" What *do* you mean? What sort of thing? Running
away from home after a fight? "

" No. This sort of dramatic thing, like making up
his mind to be unselfish when it isn't, and then leaving
a note. . . . It's the sort of thing you'd do," he added
shrewdly. " Maybe it's because you're so keen on acting."

" What a clever little boy you're getting! You'd better
go down into the yard and wash yourself under the
pump. You went to bed dirty last night. . . . As soon
as we've had breakfast and helped Mrs. H. we'll go
back to Maryknoll and spy out the land and then we'll
go on to Hereford."

" Oh, will we? I'm not so sure that we will. Maybe
I don't agree. I've never been to Hereford, except once
with Father in the vehicle, but I'm sure it's a very long
way—much too far to cycle."

Juliet jumped out of bed.

" Go on, Simon. Just be thinking of a plan to con-
found Bland and Simmonds. We're going to have fun
to-day."

Simon had no difficulty in eating the breakfast which

Mrs. Hawkins had prepared for Charles in addition to his own.

" But I did tell you," he said. " I shouted down the stairs, but I do promise you that this one hasn't been wasted."

" Truth to tell," Mrs. Hawkins said, " I heard you, but I didn't believe you. . . . How would I know that your young friend wanted to dash off like that without a meal? He was quiet, too, for I didn't hear him go."

She looked at them quizzically over the rim of her teacup.

" You're not doing anything wrong, are you? I've trusted you but there's some funny goings on it seems to me. . . . This young friend of yours with the fiddle now? What's he up to? He comes in late and runs off early without any breakfast. . . . I'm getting all bewildered and fussed. Really I am."

Juliet ran round the table and put her arm round the old lady's shoulders.

" No, Mrs. Hawkins. I promise that we haven't done anything wrong and neither has our friend. We're having a cycling holiday together and he stayed late with Mr. Bland last night to play to him, and we're going to follow him later. We've got a long way to go to-day, but before we go we want to help you, and we shall probably go to Maryknoll too. . . . Thank you a thousand times for being so kind and wonderful to us."

Simon listened to his sister with admiration. She seemed to be taking charge of the situation again and for the moment he was content. They made a good team !

Mrs. Hawkins seemed rather overcome by Juliet's appreciation, and while the latter was helping her with

the beds and the washing-up, Simon chopped firewood
for her and relaid the fire in the kitchen range. It was
still quite early when they got out their bicycles and
Juliet said:

"We'll be back soon to collect our haversacks, Mrs.
Hawkins. We're going to Maryknoll to say 'Good-bye'
and 'Thank you' to Mr. Bland. He's been *so* kind to us."

"The place looks quite nice this morning," Simon said
as they left their bicycles just inside the drive at Maryknoll ten minutes later. "What shall we do? Just go
and ring the front door bell and see what happens? What
are we going to say?"

"I don't know, yet, what we'll say. I think we'll
have to decide when we see him. If Charles is right
and Mr. Bland's keen enough on the fiddle to steal it
if he can't buy it then he'll want to know where Charles
has gone, and it's going to be our job to put him off
the scent. . . . No, Simon. I don't think we'll go to
the front door yet. . . . Let's go round to the back again
and hide in those bushes and see what's happening. If
only Bland and Simmonds are living here now, it ought
to be easy enough to keep out of sight. They can't be
everywhere at once."

The beautiful grounds looked very different in the
early morning sunshine and now that they knew that
Charles was safe the terrors of the previous night were
only a memory as they trotted quietly down the paths
between the trees to the back of the house. The back
door was open but the window of the room from which
Charles had escaped was closed. There was no sign of
Simmonds but while they were hiding behind some fruit
bushes in the kitchen garden they heard the shrilling
of the telephone bell.

" That's the telephone in his study," Simon whispered. " Do you think we could listen? Someone is sure to answer it and I think the window must be open again."

The kitchen garden seemed very open as they raced across to the little gate which led to the lawns and flower beds, but they got through safely just as the bell stopped. Stealthily they crept along the wall but as they dared not go close to the open window in daylight it was difficult to hear more than a few words—" Yes! Yes! That is certainly very satisfactory so far as your end is concerned. . . . There has, unfortunately, been a slight miscalculation here and I have yet to put my hands on the actual article. . . . No! No!! It will not take me long to do and you may certainly expect me as arranged. . . ."

They strained their ears but could hear no more, so Juliet pulled her brother back to the gate and then whispered :

" Round to the front again. I'm going to ring the bell and ask for him."

Simmonds answered the second ring and seemed surprised to see them.

" I want to speak to Mr. Bland, please," Juliet said. " It's urgent."

" He is out. Not at home," the manservant snapped.

" He is," Simon said cheekily. " We've just seen him in the garden," and by a fortunate coincidence Mr. Bland at that moment chose to take the morning air.

" Don't bother yourself," Juliet laughed. " We'll go and speak to him over there," and she turned and ran across the grass.

" Good morning, Mr. Bland," she said brightly. " Isn't it lovely? We've come for Johnny. We did come last

night at half-past nine as arranged but your Mr. Simmonds said he had never heard of him and that there
wasn't a boy here at all. It was stupid of him, wasn't it? "

" Very misguided," Mr. Bland found himself saying.

" Yes. It's silly to tell lies when the people listening
know that they're lies. How is Charles—Johnny, I
mean? Is he ready to come with us? ".

Mr. Bland of course noticed her slip at once, and the
realization that the two children knew who Charles really
was helped him to a quick decision.

" I see that you are both intelligent and sensible
children and I am indeed glad that you called this morning. I need your help badly and most particularly because I now realize that you, too, know that John Brown
is, in reality, Charles Renislau."

Juliet nodded agreement because there was no sense
in denial and Mr. Bland went on to concoct a story
which might have sounded feasible if they had not known
the truth. Glibly he explained that for some reason
Charles had run off into the darkness directly after
dinner having admitted his identity, and that Simmonds,
reluctant to disclose this information, had told them a
foolish lie.

" I naturally assumed that Charles had joined you,
my young friends, but now you tell me that you have
not seen him."

They had not told him so and Juliet did not remind
him that when he had first seen them just now he had
not asked whether Charles was with them.

" However," continued the master of Maryknoll,
looking more like Mr. Pickwick than ever, " what matters now is that he be found at once. I assure you both
that I can be of the very greatest service to Master Charles.

Indeed, I am anxious to do so, but I must find him quickly. . . . Of course you know where he lives? " he added sharply.

But Juliet was not to be caught this way. " We've never been to his home, Mr. Bland. We met him on the road and we joined up together and we liked him very much indeed. We don't really know why he wants to be called Johnny Brown but, as you guessed so cleverly just now, he did tell us his real name."

" But where does he live, girl? Where can I find him quickly? "

" Do you think he's gone home then? " Juliet asked with innocent blue eyes wide open. " How clever you are, Mr. Bland. . . . Oh, I see. You want to know where he lives when he's at home? "

Mr. Bland's neck went a little pink and he wiped his forehead with a silk handkerchief.

" Yes! That's what I want to know. WHERE DOES HE LIVE? "

" I see what you mean, sir," Simon chimed in brightly. " I'm not sure of the exact house but he did say it was Stretton way—Little Stretton or Big Stretton or Much Stretton! Some silly name, but I've forgotten which."

" Anyway," Juliet said, when she saw that this casual information had been absorbed, " I think it's jolly decent of you to be so kind to him, Mr. Bland. We like him very much but we can't spoil our holiday by waiting about for him. I expect you're right and that he's gone off home. We don't want to go north, anyway—we know all that country—but if you do find him will you please tell him that maybe we'll see him again one day? "

" Did he not tell you the name of his house? Can't you be sure of the village? "

" Sorry I can't sir, but he did say it was north of Church Stretton I think. He said, too, that they weren't on the telephone. I remember that. . . . Well, cheerio sir. Thanks very much, and we think Charles was a fool to run away. I wish you'd asked us to dinner. I wouldn't have run off I promise you."

Juliet gave him a dazzling smile and turned to wave twice to him before reaching the drive.

" Has he taken the bait, Simon? Do you think he'll go racing off towards Shrewsbury to find a house that doesn't exist? That was very bright of you, by the way. You came in very nicely. Now we've got to get on to Hereford while he goes the other way."

" And how shall we know which way he goes? "

" Listen, Simon. Will you go back to Mrs. Hawkins for the haversacks and then come and meet me at the end of the lane? I'll hide there with my bike and see if Bland comes out in his car. Can you manage the haversacks? "

" I'll try," Simon promised, " and I won't be long. Give me some money for Mrs. Hawkins, please."

It was twenty minutes before he was back and Juliet jumped out of the copse at the roadside to welcome him.

" He's gone! He's gone! Foxy Simmonds is driving him in a big, black car and hating it. They've gone to Ludlow. Now we can follow him and go south down the main road. . . . What did that sweet Mrs. Hawkins say? "

" She didn't like taking the money but I made her. She thinks we're crazy anyway and I don't blame her. Said she never knew who was going to turn up next and that she couldn't remember how many were in our party! Come on. Let's be off."

The journey south was not very eventful but they were

only a few miles from Leominster when they stopped
at a small village. It was very hot in the street now for
it was past noon, and they left their cycles in a shady
yard at the side of the general stores and went thankfully into the dark, cool interior of the shop. They were
lucky, for there were still a few ices left, some ginger
beer to put them in and straws to suck the mixture
through.

Juliet sat on a high stool with her feet tucked round
the rungs, while Simon stood in the doorway watching
the air shimmering over the hot roadway. Suddenly he
dropped his glass with a crash and backed into the
shadows of the shop.

"Hide, Juliet! Quick! Simmonds is coming down
the street on a bike."

"Don't be silly——" she began, and then when she
saw the expression on his face she jumped off the stool
and crouched down with him behind the window just
in time to see that Simon was right. The toiling, red-
faced man in unsuitable black clothes, pedalling feebly
up the village street, was undoubtedly their enemy,
Foxy. Juliet felt no pity for him. She hoped that the
temperature would rise still farther, but the fact that
he was here, on the Hereford road, was disquieting—
particularly as she had seen him driving his master in
a car not many hours ago.

As soon as he had wobbled past she jumped up:

"We must find out whether he's after us or Charles
or all of us. He's sure to ask somebody here. Can you
spy on him, Simon? I dare not because of my hair.
He'll recognize me a mile off. . . . Look! He's going
into the inn. He's left his bike outside. Could you creep
up and listen? I'll go and put our bikes out of sight in

" Look! He's going into the inn."

case he comes here and asks about us. Will you come
and find me in the yard? "

He was back in a few minutes looking very smug.

" Easy! " he boasted. " He's in the ' Sun and Harrow '
drinking pints and pints of beer and saying he's out to
find ' three kids wot 'as run away.' . . . When he's not
with people like us, Julie, he talks in that peculiar way.
. . . The other men in there are laughing at him but
none of them have seen us, and I don't think they'd
tell him if they had. We'd better get off as quickly as
we can now. We've got a good start."

" I think we'd better let him go first and then follow
him."

" That would take too long because he won't be start-
ing yet. I've taken both valves out of his tyres and stuck
K

my knife into both just to make sure. I think he'll be here for a long time."

And they went on their way rejoicing, but cycled at full speed past the open door of the " Sun and Harrow." They were the other side of the little town of Leominster when they noticed a knife-grinder, singing and grinding outside a cottage. He looked such fun and so nice and brown that Juliet smiled at him and then nearly fell off her bicycle when he winked and said, " You'll be Juliet, I reckon. I've been a'waiting for you."

" And I'm the Archbishop of Canterbury," Simon said as he dismounted. " Or should I have said Romeo? "

The pedlar winked wickedly at him too, and as the sparks flew from the long knife in his hand he told them that Charles had passed him on the road over two hours ago and had asked him to look out for them. " ' Tell her,' 'e says, ' that all goes well with me and I hope I'll see her to-night.' That's what he said, miss. . . . Good-looking lad, too, with his fiddle an' all."

" Thank you very much," Juliet replied, trying not to notice a succession of winks. " Please don't tell anyone else you've seen us, will you? "

She was very thoughtful for the next ten minutes but at last she spoke her mind.

" I'm not so sure that you were right about wrecking his bike, Simon. You see, he'll know for certain now that we're about, for nobody else would want to stop him riding a bicycle on a hot day. I'm afraid he'll telephone Mr. Bland, who I'm sure has tricked us—he must have been much cleverer than we thought—and they may both come after us now in his car."

" Unless he's riding a bike too, which is impossible," Simon added. " What do you think we ought to do? "

" Even if the knife-grinder doesn't tell anybody else that he's seen us somebody else will. Lots of people have seen us—that old chap in the grocer's shop, for instance—and they will all describe us as cycling—"

" And your hair," her brother added. " They won't forget that. You ought to cover it up."

" I know. We'll earn some more money and I'll buy a scarf. Anyhow, I think we ought to leave our bikes and go on to Hereford by bus, find Charles as soon as we can and tell him what we know."

After some argument Simon agreed and they soon found a farm just off the road where everybody was too busy to notice them. They found an old shed in the farmyard, left the cycles there and went out to wait for the bus. As soon as the familiar, single-decker, " Midland Red " drew up, Juliet jumped on the step, heaved up her haversack and then jumped off again on to Simon's foot.

" Sorry! " she mumbled to the conductor, " We don't want this bus after all. It's a mistake," and then, as it moved off, turned to her brother with scarlet cheeks. Simon, standing on one leg and rubbing one foot in his hand, wasted no words with her. " Blithering, clumsy idiot! What do you think you're doing? I'll never walk again."

" I'm sorry, Simon didn't you see him? Simmonds was sitting just by the conductor. We should have had to sit next to him. . . . When he saw us and I got off he gave me a dirty sort of sneer."

This news sobered Simon.

" We've got to find Charles first now, that's certain. You'll have to carry me, but we must get to Hereford before the bus. He must know that Simmonds is after him. . . . We should never beat the bus on our bikes, should we? "

Their problem was solved by a cheerful girl in brown dungarees, driving a baker's van. " Hop in front with me and pitch your bags in the back," she said. " I've only two more calls and we'll be back in Hereford in twenty minutes."

And so they were and no questions asked, and when they said " Good-bye " and " Thank you " to her in Widemarsh Street they were certain that they must have beaten the bus, although they had not come on the same road all the way.

" We must go to the Cathedral and find Charles at once," Juliet said, " but I must buy a scarf first. Let's see how much money we've got."

" I must have a meal," Simon protested. " We've only had snacks all day. I want two eggs on chips—and sausages too. . . . You'll have to break into your reserves. That reminds me that we haven't telephoned the parents. We must do that too. You promised."

Juliet bought a scarf—bright green—and Simon sighed as he realized that she looked just as striking with it over her blonde hair as without it. They hurried through the lovely old streets towards the softly-tinted bulk of the Cathedral with its great, square tower.

" I like this place," Simon said. " I'd like to explore it. Cathedrals always make me feel hushed and peculiar inside, but I like them. I hope Charles is here, although we're much too early."

But he was not waiting in any of the porches. Inside the clergy and choir were singing Evensong, so while Juliet sat at the back looking up at the glory and immensity of the Norman pillars and arches, Simon tiptoed up the north aisle looking to see if Charles was one of the scattered congregation. He was not there either, so he signalled to Juliet and they went out again into the sunshine, smiling at a silver-haired verger by the door.

" We've got an hour before he's due, anyway," Simon said. " Let's go and eat."

They found a café not far away and while they were waiting to be served Juliet picked up a copy of the morning's paper which had been left on the table.

" Give me the sports page," Simon said, " I want to see how Worcester are doing. . . . Don't be greedy, Julie. You can't read it all at once."

Then he noticed that his sister was too excited to do anything but point with a shaking finger at a short paragraph on the main news page.

" Look, Simon. Read this. I wonder if Charles knows? "

Over her shoulder Simon read:

FIRST PERFORMANCE IN ENGLAND

Renislau Violin Concerto at Albert Hall

" Music lovers whose memories are long enough will remember the name of the Polish composer, Alex Renislau, who has never been heard of since the destruction of Warsaw in 1939. His *Violin Concerto in C Minor* —considered to be his greatest work—which has occasionally been heard on the radio and has been performed several times on the Continent, has its first British performance in the Albert Hall, London, on Saturday evening next—a musical event of outstanding importance."

" Don't spell out the words," Juliet said excitedly as Simon grabbed the paper. " Surely you can see what this means? I wonder if Charles knows? "

" I don't suppose so, but Mr. Bland does I'm sure," Simon said. " Don't you remember that he said something about the Albert Hall and Chelsea on the telephone last night when we were listening? . . . Oh, good! Here come the eggs and chips. Let's eat as we talk. . . . I can't understand why all this is so important to Mr. Bland though."

" Perhaps the violin is specially valuable now that the concerto is going to be played in London," Juliet suggested. " Wouldn't it be wonderful to be there? But of course Charles *must* be there. We must get him to London somehow. Maybe we could go, too? "

" I knew we should want our bikes," Simon said with his mouth full. " But London is too far, anyway. . . . I wonder how Bland knew about the performance? "

" Let's go now," Juliet said. " It's nearly time and Charles must be told this news."

" He may not be there till the morning and anyway I'm still hungry. I want a good helping of a solid pudding, but of course they don't have that on now. I think I'll have some beans on toast."

She dragged him away protesting at last, but when they got back to the Cathedral there was still no sign of Charles. They walked through the peaceful cloisters, took it in turns to run round to each of the doors at intervals in case they had missed him and at last, in despair, walked down to the lovely bridge across the Wye.

For a few minutes they leaned over the parapet from one of the triangular refuges and watched the water swirling round the cut-waters of the six arches.

" I'm worried, Simon. We *must* find him. He's here somewhere I'm sure, but we've nowhere to stay to-night and at any moment I'm afraid Simmonds may turn up. We must be careful not to be seen by him. He couldn't have found Charles already, could he? "

As she was speaking the last words she felt a hand on her arm—a hand which was not her brother's for he was on her other side with his arms on the stone parapet.

She felt herself go cold with fear. So Simmonds had found them after all! Then a quiet, gentle voice said:

" I think you must be Juliet Buckingham? " and she turned to see a kind-faced, silver-haired old man dressed in black, standing just behind her.

" Yes, I am. Who are you? I think I've seen you before? "

He smiled slowly.

" Many people see me. My name is Messenger and I am one of the vergers of the Cathedral. I have a message for you. . . . I was to tell you that your friend, Charles, has gone on to the fair because he has seen someone by the strange name of Foxy. He suggests that you go and find him and is sorry he was not able to meet you at the North Door. If you do not find him he will be coming back to my cottage—the third on the left back there, with clematis over the porch—later to play to me and my dear wife. You two will be welcome also."

Juliet grabbed his old black jacket with both hands and laughed up at him.

" Thank you! Thank you, Mr. Messenger. We were worried about Charles. How did you find us? "

" I have been looking for you. I saw you pass my

window. . . . I am sure you will find him. I think I might say that he spoke very—very warmly—of you both. . . . We shall hope to see you later," and with a courtly little bow he turned away.

"There you are," Simon said. "Why worry? Something always turns up. Let's get on to the fair, although I wish we could dump these haversacks somewhere. . . . Listen!"

A little breeze from the south fanned their faces, and brought with it a refreshing smell of water meadows and running water. It brought with it, too, the cheerful and unmistakable sound of the music of a roundabout.

CHAPTER 8

ROUNDABOUT

" WHAT do you think of that? " Simon said as their new friend, Mr. Messenger, wandered back towards his cottage. " Now that I've had a little something to eat, and I know that Charles is about somewhere, there's nothing that I'd enjoy more than a fair! Let's go, Julie."

" Yes, I know all about that, Simon. I'd like a fair too, but Charles is really very trying. However are we going to find him at a fair? Why didn't he leave a better message than that? "

" I don't suppose he'd got the time. Maybe he saw that Foxy was on his trail and had to run for it. I think it was smart of him to think of leaving a message with that verger chap and, after all, a place where there are a lot of people is always a good place to hide, isn't it? I'm going to enjoy looking for him. We can try everything in the fair until we do find him. Come on! "

" All right. I do hope nothing awful has happened to him. I wish I knew where Foxy is now. . . . Simon! I've just had an awful thought. We haven't written or telephoned the parents yet. Do you think they're worrying? "

" I shouldn't think so. I think Father might worry a bit if we ring up and ask for some money, and we may have to do that. I've got a feeling that we're going to spend a lot to-night. Shall we share what you've got now and spend it as we like? "

Juliet soon disabused him of this idea and then they

hoisted their haversacks on to their backs and trudged over the bridge towards the gay clamour of the roundabout.

There was no need to ask the way to the fair for now that the day's work was over and dusk was beginning to fall, hundreds of laughing, chattering people were making their way towards a glow in the sky about half a mile from the city. Although many fairs make a pretence of opening up in an afternoon, they offer usually only a travesty of an entertainment in daylight. A real fair is rather like one of those rare and extravagant flowers that only bloom when day is done, and so it was with Hereford's, which always arrived on the last Thursday in July. After rather apologetically opening a few stalls and hand-turned roundabouts for babies, it only came to life when the naphtha lights flared and brought the crowds; when the brazen music from the roundabouts drowned the shouts of the men and women at the booths, and when the excited riders in the dodgems screamed as the sparks crackled and flew and the cars collided.

It was not quite dusk when Juliet and Simon reached the big meadow where the fair was flaunting itself, but the music and the lights had laid their spell on them for the last five minutes and when they arrived they were hot and breathless.

" If only we dared leave these haversacks somewhere," Simon gasped. " It will be difficult to have fun with them on."

The fairground was triangular with the entrance at the narrow end, but round the edges of the field, behind the booths and tents, the caravans, cars, lorries and trailers of the showmen were crowded together, and in this shadowy hinterland chickens squawked, mongrel dogs barked and little girls carried babies almost as big as themselves.

The Buckinghams stood, for a moment, on the edge of delight. The fair was warming up! Two girls wearing paper hats bearing the invitation "Kiss me," ran past screaming. Against the darkening sky a tinted plume of smoke from the little chimney on the roof of a roundabout sailed like a feather in the evening breeze. Below the canopied roof, the brightly-coloured horses glowed in the lights of the lamps and careered gaily round and round to the loud and lilting music. Men were shouting, children calling and girls laughing, but louder than the clamour of human voices was the thudding clangour of the roundabouts' brazen song. In one corner the dodgems dodged and collided. In another a man in a top-hat beat a drum and yelled a raucous invitation outside the boxing tent. Rifles cracked as old soldiers cheerfully spent many shillings in an attempt to win a hideous china ornament worth only a few pence! Handsome gipsy women, with gleaming rings in their ears, were luring even the most cautious to roll a penny across the chequered, sloping boards or to toss cane rings over prizes which looked too garish to be true. In one dark corner strange, oblong shapes swung up against the sky, blotted out a few stars and then slid into the gloom again.

Juliet sighed ecstatically and pulled the green scarf from her head.

"It's wonderful, Simon. Shall we start on the swing boats? They make me feel awful, but it's worth it, and we ought to go high with these heavy haversacks."

"All right. I don't mind. Will you do chair-o-planes with me next?"

" No. I can't face them. I swore I'd never do them
again after last year. My stomach moves about and everything goes round me instead of me going round them,
if you know what I mean? "

" Perfectly ! " Simon grinned. " For an actress
and mistress of English I think you're wonderful.
Come on ! "

There was not much time during the next half-hour
to remember Charles, although once Juliet, in full cry
on a spotted horse on the roundabout, thought she saw
him in the crowd. Her piercing cry of " Chaaarles ! "
was drowned in the blare of the mechanical organ and
the only one who heard her was a grinning man in a
blue jersey and rubber shoes, who was dodging between
the horses collecting sixpences.

She found Charles when she least expected to do so.
Simon was swinging far out into the dusk over the booths
and crowds in a chair-o-plane, while she waited for him
at the corner of the rifle range. Several people stumbled
against the haversacks at her feet so she moved back a
few paces into the shadows, turned round to see where
she was and recognized Charles sitting on the steps of
a caravan. He was looking very handsome and without
a care in the world as he talked and laughed with a
gipsy girl of about eleven, who was leaning against the
steps at his side. Juliet was suddenly very angry with
him. She may even have been a little jealous, but it
was infuriating to see him enjoying himself after leaving
for them a vague message and causing them no end of
trouble ever since he had run away from Honeysuckle
Cottage. Then she remembered that if she wasn't careful she would lose her brother, and as Charles looked
set for hours she turned back as the chair-o-planes slowed

down. Simon reeled a little as he came over and certainly looked a trifle pale.

"Oh! Charles?" he said. "I'd forgotten about him. Where is he? I can't go on those again now, I suppose?"

Juliet had a shrewd idea that a second trip was the last thing he really wanted, but all that she did was to grab his arm and lead him through the gap between the booths so that he could see the caravan.

Charles was still enjoying himself and, what was even more annoying, greeted them both without the slightest apology for leading them half across one county into another!

"Hullo, you two. I thought you'd turn up. It was a good idea to leave the message with Old Faithful, wasn't it?"

They stared at him without speaking but he remained in the very best of spirits.

"As soon as I heard there was to be a fair here I thought it would be the place for us—for me, anyway —and then I saw 'you-know-who' prowling round and that settled it. . . . It's nice to see you again, Juliet. Did you have a decent journey?"

"A lovely, beautiful journey, thank you Charles. There was never a dull moment in it. We never had a worry and that must have been because you made everything so easy for us."

There was an edge to her voice that warned him, at last, that all was not well, so he got off the steps of the caravan and came over.

"Sorry about dashing off like that this morning, but you've no idea how thrilled I am that you've both come. I didn't want to drag you into trouble but I didn't want to lose you, either. Where can we talk?"

" That's all right, Charles. But who's your new friend? "

Charles smiled in his easy way.

" New friend? Oh, this kid? Miranda! Come and meet Juliet and Simon."

The gipsy may not have been very old in years but the look she gave Juliet was not very youthful. She came forward a few steps, dismissed Simon with a brief glance and then the two girls smiled at each other rather like two wolves.

" We've got a lot to tell you, Charles, and there's no time to waste. Let's find a place where we can talk privately," Juliet said. " Ask this little girl to look after our haversacks for a bit, will you? We're sick of carrying them round."

Miranda obviously did not care for the reference to her size and age, but Charles seemed to have cast a spell over her and when he said, " We'll be back soon, Miranda. Take care of this luggage for us like a sport," she took the haversacks into the caravan and then watched the others wander off among the lorries and trailers behind the booths.

" She's all right," Charles explained. " Her mother and father run the chair-o-planes. I've had a couple of free rides already. . . . Before you tell me all your news, though, have you seen Foxy? "

" Have we seen Foxy—? " Simon began indignantly. " We've hardly seen any one else. Has he seen you, 'cos he knows we're on our way to Hereford? "

" I don't think so. I spotted him prowling round the Cathedral but I don't think he saw me. I've been dodging about the town a lot but I didn't dare wait for you where I'd said, so I left that message with the old boy and came on here. . . . Now tell me what you've been doing? "

" There's such a lot and we've got the most exciting news for you, Charles. Have you seen a paper to-day? " Juliet said.

" No. I don't often look at papers. Only the cricket. What's happened? "

" Just a sec. before we show you. Where can we go and talk? There's such a muddle round here and everybody is staring at us. . . . If Foxy is about by any chance I suppose it would be safer for us to be with the crowds inside the fair."

They found a fairly peaceful corner by the boxing tent and it was here that they told him of their adventures and of how Bland had undoubtedly tricked them and sent Foxy south on a bicycle while he was probably searching the country towards Stretton in his car.

" But now that Foxy has seen us and may have recognized you he's sure to have let his master know somehow or other," Juliet explained. " They've been much too clever for us, Charles, and this is specially important because of what we found in to-day's paper. Show him, Simon! "

Charles read the cutting twice and when he looked up his eyes were shining.

" I can't believe it," he said. " It's almost the most wonderful thing that could happen. I must go to London at once, of course, and I must let Mother know somehow. . . . This alters everything. You do see that I must be there, don't you? Would you two come with me? It would be grand if you would. After my mother there's nobody in the world I'd rather have there than you two."

And for that remark Juliet forgave him everything.

" Of course we'll come. We'll manage it somehow, but try not to be so excited, Charles, and let's think carefully what's best to do. . . . The concert is Saturday and this is Thursday night, so I don't see how we're going to get there without a lot more money. We can't cycle and anyway Simon and I left our bikes behind in a village, when we saw Foxy on the bus. We might hitch-hike, but don't you think you ought to telephone your uncle and let him know about this? You did say he wasn't too bad and I'm sure he'd help you now. Of course, if you'd rather not do that I'm sure my parents would help—lend us some money, I mean."

Before Charles could answer Simon shouted something and dashed between two booths into the crowds.

Juliet and Charles stared at each other in astonishment.

" Is he often taken like that? " the latter asked. " What did he say? "

" I couldn't hear. I thought it was, ' Stay there.' What shall we do? "

" You stay here unless he comes back and I'll go and look for him."

" Oh no you don't. You'll get lost then and I'll be looking for both of you. . . . Let's go and find him together."

This was not at all a good idea but they did not realize how stupid they had been until they had been pushed and jostled about for ten minutes without a hope of finding anyone special. They soon lost their sense of direction and finally Juliet lost her temper.

" This is the most ridiculous, idiotic, unpractical way of searching for anybody that I can think of. I'm furious with Simon and I don't think you're very bright either, Charles. None of this would have happened if you hadn't dashed off like a make-believe hero from Honeysuckle Cottage this morning. I'm sick of this and I've got a headache. . . . For goodness sake suggest something sensible, Charles—and the next lout that treads on my sandals is going to get kicked. . . . Can't you think of *anything*? "

" Yes, I can. Let's stand right here where Simon can't help seeing us if he really is looking for us. If we stay here long enough he'll find us. . . . I'll have something to say to him when he does turn up, too. Little idiot, dashing off like that and upsetting and worrying us."

Juliet raised her chin and looked into the distance over his shoulder.

" I'm not upset or worried, thank you, and I'm quite sure that Simon had a very good reason for dashing off like that."

Both of them were right, for Simon did see them first and his reason for running off was important if not particularly sensible.

" I thought I'd lost you both as well," he gasped as he pushed through the crowd to them. " Why didn't you stay where I left you? We've wasted too much time already."

Juliet grabbed him by the arm. His face, although very pale, was wet with perspiration and he looked both worried and frightened.

" Buck up, Simon. Tell us. Why did you dash off like that? "

" Foxy! I saw Foxy Simmonds with that kid, Miranda, from the caravan. You were just talking to Charles about money or something, and I was watching the people pass the gap between those two stands when I saw them. I'm certain about it. Absolutely positive,

L

although it doesn't make much sense to me. He was bending down talking to her, but when I dashed out some fools got in my way and I lost them. I've been searching in the fair and among the caravans outside, but I just can't see them, and then I lost myself as well. I thought that if only one of us went after him we might have a chance of following him properly. Three is too many to trail someone as suspicious as Foxy. . . . What's the matter, Charles? You're looking awful."

" I feel it. I've done the most terrible thing. Quick! We've got to find Miranda's caravan. Where are the chair-o-planes? "

" But *why*, Charles? What's wrong? "

" Can't you see that Foxy has fooled me too? I thought he hadn't seen me in the town but he must have done. He's followed me here and must have seen me leave the fiddle in the caravan, and now he's gone after that kid, Miranda."

Breathless and frightened they pushed their way to the corner where the chair-o-planes were still sailing over the heads of the crowd. Charles charged up the steps of the caravan and pushed open the door.

In a minute he was back.

" It's gone. Your haversacks are still there but the fiddle has gone. He's stolen it for that old beast, Bland. What a fool I am. I ought never to have left it there. . . . And Miranda's not there, either."

" Here she comes now," Juliet said suddenly. " I think she'll have something very interesting to tell us."

Miranda was sucking a toffee apple and although her sticky face brightened when she first caught sight of Charles, her eyes filled with tears when he grabbed her arm and almost shouted :

*" It's gone! Your haversacks are still there but the
fiddle has gone."*

"Where's the fiddle? You promised me that you'd
look after it and that I could trust you. Where is it?"

She wrenched herself free and ran up into the caravan,
but they knew before she came back with a white and
stricken face that Charles was right and that Foxy had
been too clever for them all.

"It was there," the girl began. "I swear it was. . . ."

"We know that," Simon snapped. "Who was that
man in black whispering to you, and where is he now?
He's the chap who has taken the fiddle."

As soon as she realized that she had failed Charles,
Miranda burst into tears and set up a bitter wailing
that shocked them all. While the two boys stood by

helplessly Juliet went across to her, put an arm round her shoulder and tried to comfort her.

" Listen, Miranda. We know you're sorry. We've got to find that man quickly, so please tell us everything that happened to you after we went off. . . . But do please be quick."

Miranda's story was simple enough. Almost as soon as the others had gone off Foxy had come up to her, and after describing Charles as his friend, had asked whether he had still got his fiddle safe. Miranda had reassured him and told him where it was, and then Foxy had persuaded her to come with him into the crowds.

" He kep' on lookin' over his shoulder when he was a'talkin' to me 'ere. . . . Seemed to think somethink was be'ind 'im. . . . But 'e was a nice enough gent to me then, all the same, but he was a bit rum."

" Go on," Juliet coaxed, " Why was he so rum? "

Miranda explained that almost as soon as she had led him past the chair-o-planes into the fair he seemed to want to go somewhere else.

" Then 'e said 'e'd got to find you first, but would I please go back up the road a bit to a letter-box and post a letter 'e'd forgot. 'E give me the letter, and ten bob too, and I done it and come back and 'ere I am, and I know there was nothin' wrong in takin' the money or 'elping 'im. . . . 'Ow would I know? "

No doubt it had been easy enough to get her out of the way so that he could slip into the empty caravan and steal the fiddle. Almost too easy, Charles reflected bitterly, as Miranda went on to confess that Foxy had asked about Juliet and Simon and that she had said that the three had gone off together.

" Oh well," Juliet said. " That's done it. We're not

nearly so smart as we thought we were! I feel like a balloon when the air has been let out of it."

"You look like it," her brother said rudely. "Let's get out of this row. I suppose you realize that we've got nowhere to sleep to-night and I'm so tired that I can hardly stand up. Give me our haversacks, Miranda, unless you've let Foxy take those as well."

Charles leaned back against the wheels of the painted caravan with misery in his face. He was tired and unhappy and did not know what to do next. Somehow he must get to London to hear his father's concerto. Somehow he must let his mother know about it and somehow he must get back the stolen violin, even if he had to admit complete defeat by telling the police and going back to Manlands. He had very little money, which did not make any of the problems easier to solve, and as he tried to puzzle them out the thud and rhythm of the roundabouts' song beat into his tired head, the crowds still laughed and shouted, while the showmen bellowed their invitations.

Then he felt a hand slipped into his arm. Juliet was looking down at her dusty sandals and he had to stoop close to her gleaming head to hear what she was saying.

"Don't worry, Charles. We'll find a way out. We'll do something together. There's three of us and lots more behind us and we'll get your fiddle back and get to London too. . . . Let's go now. I can't stand this noise. Let's go and plan what's best to do."

Without a word they left Miranda at the caravan steps. Charles heaved Juliet's haversack on to his own back as Simon led them past the clutter of caravans and lorries to the road. As they trudged back towards the city they met many who were only now on the way to the fair. It was quite dark now, and as they crossed the Wye Bridge Juliet turned back for a moment to look at the great glow in the sky and listen to the echo of the roundabouts' song.

Then, " Where are we going? " she said dully.

" To the verger's cottage, of course. My bike is there. What a fool I was not to leave the fiddle there too. I expect they'll give us something to eat and let us sit down somewhere and talk, anyway. What shall we do, Juliet? "

" Everything is better when you've had a meal," Simon said. " I bet we don't worry so much when we're not so hungry. Here's the cottage. Clematis on the porch he said."

The grave-faced Mr. Messenger answered their knock almost immediately.

" I hoped that you would all return together. This has saved me a great deal of trouble. . . . Come in, please. Someone is waiting to see you."

He stood aside as Juliet stepped into the tiny hall.

" To see *me*? " she stammered.

" To see you all. . . . In the parlour, if you please."

He opened another door and closed it immediately the three children had crossed the threshold. For a moment they stood blinking in the glare of the strong light, and then Juliet felt her knees go weak and flopped down on the nearest chair. The Messengers' parlour was very small and very full of furniture and ornaments, but everything in it now was dwarfed by the figure of the large policeman standing with his back to the fireplace.

CHAPTER 9

POLICE

" WELL! Well! " said the large policeman. " Three little
birds all come home to the same nest at the same time,
but it's the bird by the door I reckon that we're most interested in. . . . Very, very interested in birds the police
gets sometimes. Specially birds what fly away from their
own nests like cuckoos—"

" Nonsense," Juliet said, recovering from the first
shock of surprise. " You know perfectly well that cuckoos
don't have nests. Please don't think I meant to be rude
but you are a great shock to us and I know perfectly well
that cuckoos don't have nests. That's just their trouble—"

" *Just* a minute. Just a minute, young lady? " The
policeman glared down condescendingly at the girl who
had dared to interrupt him. " Never you mind about
cuckoos! I must ask you just to keep silent for a while.
It's the young gentleman by the door I'm anxious to have
a word with."

" Now don't you bully him," Juliet said. " We're
all in this together. . . . Well. When I say ' this,' I
mean we're having a holiday together and—"

Charles, who was looking very pale and grim, stepped
forward and said:

" All right, Juliet. Thanks all the same but I'll tell
the constable anything he wants to know and then we've
got plenty to tell him."

" That's more like it," P.C. Perkins said approvingly
and pulled his notebook from his tunic pocket. " Your

name, if you please, my lad, and where have you come
from? "

Charles knew now that it was no use concealing his
identity, particularly as he had made up his mind that he
was going to telephone Hetty to-night to see if a letter
had come from his mother. Even if Bland had sent the
police after him with the suggestion that he had stolen
his own father's violin, the truth was the only thing
which would count now!

" Charles Renislau is my name and I live with my
uncle, Mr. Martin Strong at Manlands. I left there the
day before yesterday—or yesterday, very early really
—for a sort of cycling holiday, and joined up with these
two friends at Ludlow. . . . But why do you want me? "

P.C. Perkins snapped his notebook and smiled broadly.
They all smiled willingly at him in return, feeling that
they had passed through a storm into sunshine.

" *Very* good! I must ask you, young gentleman, just
to accompany me to the police station to confirm what
you say to Sergeant Smithson. Your uncle, Mr. Strong,
is most anxious to locate you and you can speak to him
on the telephone from the station, and the sooner the
better," and he shifted his weight so that his belt creaked.

Simon, who for the last few minutes had been perched
uncomfortably on the edge of the sofa, could contain
himself no longer.

" Hi! That's all very well, but what about us? What
about us Buckinghams? If you're going to take Charles
to the police station we're jolly well coming too. I've
always wanted to do that. . . . Come on, Julie. Don't sit
there grinning like that. There's nothing to laugh at.
. . . *And there's another thing,*" he almost shouted as
he got up, " What about Foxy stealing the violin from

the caravan? Aren't we going to do something about that? . . . Come on! We've got more to say to the sergeant than he can have to say to us."

The party moved into the tiny hall but before they went out Charles, Juliet and P.C. Perkins tried to explain to the bewildered Mr. and Mrs. Messenger that nobody was going to be arrested and that no shame would fall upon their cottage.

"But where will you be sleeping to-night?" asked Mrs. Messenger, who was unexpectedly plump and jolly. "That is if they let you out of the station."

Charles took control.

"My fiddle has been stolen at the fair," he explained, "so I shan't be able to play to you, but if we could come back and camp out somewhere we should be grateful. I expect we shall be off very early in the morning, but we'll be glad to tidy up and we'll do any jobs for you with pleasure."

"Come back? Of course you will. Glad to see you all—except you, Constable Perkins, of course. There's no room for you and three children in this house at the same time. . . . Now don't you go a'bullying of them, Mr. Policeman. It's late and they ought to be in bed. . . . You youngsters can leave your luggage here."

There were still people about the streets as the constable led them to the police station and the impression given to many of the curious passers-by was that of an ocean liner accompanied by three fussy tugs.

"What I should like to know, if it's not a police secret," Simon said, "is how you came to Mr. Messenger's to find us—or Charles, I mean, because I know you're not interested in us."

P.C. Perkins explained that when Mr. Strong asked

the police to help him to find Charles immediately, he not only described his appearance, but explained that he was very musical and would probably try to earn money by playing his violin.

" That were quite a lot to go on," he went on, " and when I were put on the job it seemed to me that any lad interested in music and the like would go to the Cathedral sooner or later, so down there I goes and calls on old Harry Messenger to ask if he'd seen you. He had, o' course, and hearing as you'd all gone to the fair but were coming back to his place, I thought I'd as soon rest me feet in Harry's parlour as wear 'em out down in the meadow searching for you. . . . And now here we are, and you'll remember to speak respectfully to Sergeant, young shaver, and then you can telephone your uncle that you're safe and sound."

" But we must see the sergeant, too," Juliet protested. " I adore sergeants, and we must tell him about Foxy."

" All in good time, my dear. . . . One thing at a time is our motto here. One thing at a time and do it proper. Sit you down here. . . . Come you with me, young Charles."

" I'll tell them all about Foxy," Charles said over his shoulder. " Wait for me."

Almost as soon as Charles and P.C. Perkins had disappeared into an inner room, Juliet nudged her brother violently and they both got up off the bench and went to the door.

A policeman at his desk looked up and Juliet decided, correctly, that he had no sense of humour.

" We shall be back in ten minutes. We are going to a call box. We are not running away," she explained, and before he could answer they ran out into the dark.

" I'm very disappointed in the police," Simon said. " I'm sure they're kind but they seem jolly slow about detecting. Why don't they get moving after Foxy? They won't even let us tell them about him! What do we want a call box for, anyway? . . . Or do we? "

" Of course. I'm going to telephone the parents. I've got an idea that Father will be interested in all this. It's a wonderful story for him, Simon, and I think he might like to do something about it—with us, I mean."

Simon looked at her admiringly.

" You ring him then. It's nearly eleven, and I suppose you'll reverse the call? "

She did this, not as a matter of course, but because the fair had proved to be rather expensive. With Simon crowded against her in the stuffy call box she felt a little thrill when her father's loved and familiar voice came over the wire.

" That must be my daughter. I only wish I had the strength of mind to refuse the call. How are you, darling, and where are you? "

" We're all right, Daddy, thank you. We've got some news, though. . . . We're in Hereford. We've just left the police station and we're going back there in a minute. . . ."

The pause at the other end was only just perceptible. He was a wonderful father!

" Of course. Quite a natural place for you to be. I suppose they've just let you out for a few minutes to ask for bail or something. What have you been doing? "

" We haven't been doing anything except have the most incredible adventures. Listen, Daddy, because what I'm telling you is real and true. That boy, John Brown, is really Charles Renislau, the son of a famous Polish composer, and that fiddle he had was his father's. His mother is in Switzerland and he ran away from his uncle's place where he lives because he detests his cousins—"

" An excellent reason," Mr. Buckingham murmured. " Is he still with you? In that call box, perhaps? "

" No! No! He's at the police station too. He's being questioned now. . . . No. *Please* don't keep interrupting, Daddy. This really is most terrifically exciting and it is all really true. You said we should find adventures if we went out after them and we certainly have. . . . Are you still there? . . . Oh, good! Listen. Because Charles—that's John Brown—ran away from home his uncle has rung up the police and they've just found him, and we were with him at a fair." . . .

" Stop! Stop! " Mr. Buckingham shouted so that Simon jumped in surprise. " I can't stand it! Just tell me plainly whether you and Simon are really all right and not in any trouble. Tell me that first."

" Very well, Daddy. We are."

" All right or in trouble? "

" All right and not in trouble, thank you, but we want you to come and see us in Hereford to-morrow morning in the vehicle. We want to tell you everything and we want you to help us to get Charles' fiddle back because we don't think the police will be much good at it." . . . Here she paused for breath and her father rushed into the breach.

" Why can't they? And what's happened to his fiddle? "

" Haven't I told you a million times? It's been stolen —yes, STOLEN—by a man called Foxy who works for another man who ran a fête in his garden who wants

the fiddle. . . . You do understand, don't you, darling?
. . . No. Don't interrupt me, *please*. The most
important thing of all is that the violin concerto which
Charles' dead father wrote is being performed for the
first time in England at the Albert Hall on Saturday,
and Charles wants us all to be there with him. . . . Will
you come to-morrow? Do, Daddy. We'll meet you at
eight o'clock at the cross roads of High Street and Broad
Street and tell you everything. We really need you,
Daddy, and you asked us to let you know if we did.
You will be there, won't you? It's a grand idea for a
story for you I promise."

" It's clear that I must come if only to get you out
of the police station. Is that where you're both sleeping
to-night? "

" Oh no, darling. We're sleeping with one of the
vergers of the Cathedral. . . . At least—we hope we are."

A groan came over the wire.

" You're mad, my children. I shall never dare tell
your mother all that you tell me. Try and keep out
of more trouble until I see you in the morning. . . . Is
Simon there? I'd like to assure myself that his mental
state is better than yours."

Simon took up the hot receiver.

" Hullo, Father! I know it sounds crazy but everything Julie has said is true. I'm jolly glad you're coming
but we want you to know that we are managing like
you told us and I've earned some money. . . . Oh, well.
I'll tell you to-morrow. Cheerio! "

" Oh dear," Juliet gasped as they staggered out into
the fresh air, " I do hope he understands. I couldn't
have been plainer I know, but sometimes I think I'm
better just talking to people close by than on the tele-

phone. . . . Look, here's Charles coming to meet us."

" Has he got handcuffs on? " Simon said. " I vote we go back to Clematis Cottage and see if they've got an old pigsty or something where we can sleep. We don't seem to have had a decent night's rest for ages. . . . Hullo, Charles. I s'pose they want to see us now, don't they? "

" Not a bit," Charles replied. " They're not interested in either of you or my stolen fiddle. I can't make them see sense."

" Are you free again? " Juliet asked dramatically.

" Oh yes. I'm free. But I've got to go back home. I've spoken to Uncle—but I'll tell you all about that when we're back at the Messengers'."

And with that the impatient Buckinghams were forced to be content, for there was no doubt that Charles was feeling temperamental. Juliet was tired too, and almost wept when Mrs. Messenger proved to be so kind and gave them such a welcome. The hospitality she so generously provided was limited and simple, and after showing them where they could wash and sleep, the charming old couple left them alone in the kitchen.

" I wonder if we shall be able to keep up this sort of thing every night," Simon said as he bit into a big slice of bread and jam. " We're lucky with our cottages so far. I like them."

" I don't suppose we shall," Juliet replied. " Suppose you buck up, Charles, and tell us exactly what's happened to you. . . . You're not being very friendly."

" I'm sorry. It's just that I'm so miserable. I've lost my violin and now I've got to go back to Manlands. I shall lose the two best friends I've ever had and I don't suppose I'll get to London by Saturday."

" But if you explain about your father's concerto surely your uncle will help you to go there? You *must* go! "

" He sounded quite decent on the telephone, but when I told him about Saturday he just said we'd have to see about that."

" You've run away once," Simon said encouragingly, " why don't you do it again if you're not sure whether he'll help? Our father is coming to Hereford for us in the car at eight o'clock to-morrow morning. He's all right. Of course he thinks he's going to take us home, but he's not. If the police won't help you about the fiddle we're going to find Foxy somehow and then we've all got to be at the Albert Hall on Saturday, so maybe he'll take us."

Charles looked at them gloomily.

" You might have told me you were going to do that. Anyway, I've promised Uncle that I'll go home first thing in the morning and I can't break that promise. There's another thing, too. I found out that there's a letter from my mother waiting for me. It's marked ' Urgent ' and I must get back to see that."

Juliet yawned inelegantly. She did not like Charles quite as much in his present mood, but she could see that he was very worried.

" Very well, then," she said. " I'm sorry I didn't tell you I was going to telephone home. I really promised to do that every day, but you were stuck in the ridiculous police station with a lot of pompous policemen who didn't seem interested in what we'd done or were willing to do. If you've got to go home first thing to-morrow morning and the police here don't show a bit more interest in Foxy and Bland, we shall persuade Father to help us trace Foxy. I'm not going to give up the adventure as easily as all that. Are you, Simon? . . . Oh! He's asleep, poor lad. . . . He's not going to give up, anyhow, I can promise you that. . . . I'm too tired to make any new plans now, but everything will be different in the morning. You won't run off again, will you, Charles? It's such a nuisance chasing you all over the country."

"No, I won't do that. Julie? I was wondering whether perhaps your father would take me home to Manlands in his car as soon as he arrives. I must see this letter from my mother as quickly as possible and otherwise I suppose I shall have to cycle."

Juliet got up and yawned again.

"I must say that I think you've got a cheek, Charles. It seems to me that you're not nearly so interested in this adventure as you were, for all your fine talk. If this old fiddle that you say once belonged to your father is really important to you I can't think why you don't do more about it, instead of dashing off home when your uncle rings up a policeman."

"What do you mean?"

"Just that. Your uncle knows where you are now and you told me that you hate your two cousins so much that you're not going back until you've proved yourself independent. Why didn't you tell him that you've got to find the fiddle first and make him realize how important that is? I can't understand you, Charles. I do hope you're not feeble. . . . Tuck little Simon up on the sofa. I'm going to bed. Good-night.

Charles was not used to being spoken to like this— particularly by a girl—and he sat on thoughtfully for a long time after Juliet had tiptoed upstairs.

Meanwhile, Simon snored gently with his head on the opposite side of the table and made little complaint beyond a grunt and a grumble when Charles heaved him into an easy chair, pulled off his shoes for him and switched out the light.

In addition to all his other troubles Charles was beginning to wish that he could sleep on a bed again, but he was very tired and after tossing and turning for a long hour he did not wake when Juliet crept into the parlour soon after seven next morning to wake her brother.

Simon was never at his best in the early morning and it needed all Juliet's tact and persuasion to get him back to consciousness and out of the house.

" Do buck up, Simon. . . . Of course you must wash! Don't be such a baby, and don't make a noise and wake up those nice Messengers. . . . This is the bathroom. It's very small and I can't think how they manage. Don't use their towel, idiot! . . . No. I can't get at mine in the haversack either. Just splosh your face and come out wet. That's what I had to do." . . .

" It's not fair, Julie. If you were a boy I'd bash you for getting me up like this. Just because you're my sister you think you can boss me about and get up at unearthly hours. . . ."

" Have you forgotten that we're meeting Daddy and that we've got to do something about Charles' fiddle? Charles is going to be too feeble to do anything himself I'm sure and we've got to show him how to set about it."

" Oh! I see. I'd forgotten about that. Come on, then. Does Charles know we're going to meet the parent? "

" Yes. I told him last night. We'll come back later

M

and wake him up and give the Messengers a hand, and
then we'll make Father take us out to breakfast."

" We're much too early," Simon grumbled as they
tiptoed down the stairs. " You might have let me sleep
on," but he cheered up when they were out in the morning sunshine.

" Was Father very annoyed about being asked to get
up so early and come here to see us? " he said when
they reached the cross roads in the centre of the city.

" I thought he was wonderful," Juliet said. " He really
is most understanding. Simon! You know that he'll
want to find out everything about Foxy and Bland and
the fiddle and the police. You'll back me up, won't
you, and try and make him understand that we've got
to find the fiddle and get to London by to-morrow night.
. . . I think we shall have rather a job."

" So do I. . . . I'm bored with waiting. Let's try and
see what's behind some of these shop blinds."

They wandered up the street, peered into doorways,
and then found a newspaper shop open. They divided
the paper—Simon taking the sports pages—and strolled
back towards the cross roads. Juliet was reprimanded by
a man on his way to work for not looking where she
was going, and just as she apologized and put down
her share of the paper a low, black car swept by very
fast on the other side of the road.

" Simon! " she gasped, " Did you see him? That was
Bland driving that black car with Foxy in the back.
I'm sure of it. I couldn't mistake them."

Simon dropped the sports pages.

" That's done it! I suppose Foxy telephoned and told
him that he'd got the fiddle and that Bland has come

*She wrenched open the door of the old car and kissed
her father.*

over to fetch him. We'll never catch him now. What
shall we do?"

"Here's Daddy," Juliet yelled and rushed into the
road waving her arms. "Darling! It's wonderful of
you to come like this." She wrenched open the door of
the old car and kissed her father. "Listen! You haven't
got a second to spare. That man, Bland, who has stolen
Charles' fiddle is just a minute or two ahead of you in
a big black car. . . . Go after him, darling, and catch
him. . . . Jump in, Simon. . . . We think he'll go to
London, and Ross is the right road isn't it? HURRY!
HURRY! . . . We'll give you all the news as we go."

Mr. Buckingham backed away from his exuberant
daughter and switched off the engine.

"Good morning, Simon," he then said. "How are
you? Juliet has done all the talking so far."

" I'm very well, thank you Father, and we're very pleased to see you, but I'm afraid you will have to go very fast now to catch the black car. Do you think the vehicle will stand it? "

" I have only the remotest idea what you're both talking about. There are hundreds of thousands of black cars in this country and I have never seen this Mr. Bland in my life. I have left your mother and my home at an unreasonable hour, and have squandered precious petrol to come here just to assure myself that you are both still in your right senses and that the police are not really after you. I cannot and will not race off after a car looking like thousands of others until you explain yourselves clearly. . . . Why, Juliet, my dear. You're crying! What's wrong? "

" I'm not really. It's just that you don't understand how terribly vital all this is. . . . We really mean it, darling. This is serious. We must follow that man, get back the fiddle and be in the Albert Hall in London with Charles to-morrow evening."

Her father sat back and mopped his forehead.

" Very well. I can see you're serious. I cannot catch that car now, and I daresay ten more minutes won't make much difference. Just tell me, Juliet—and don't interrupt, Simon—everything that has happened since you went which affects the position this morning. . . . And don't snivel, my darling. Here's my grubby old handkerchief and we'll get this sorted out somehow."

Juliet gulped, kissed the top of his head and told him everything as coherently as she possibly could. He only asked a few questions and Simon, fidgeting about on the back seat, never interrupted once.

" Right! " Mr. Buckingham said when she had

finished. " That was told as well as an author's daughter should tell a story. . . . I like your adventure, children, and we'll go after Mr. Septimus Bland. I think I'd like to meet him. But first to your verger for courtesy's sake and to pick up your luggage and to see Charles. Show me the way."

Charles was in the porch, scowling up the street when they drove up. Mr. Buckingham smiled at him and then went straight in to thank the Messengers and settle up with them.

" He's going after Bland ! " Simon whispered hoarsely. " We've just seen him in a car with Foxy driving towards London. We're going to chase him and get your fiddle back, 'cos we don't think it worth waiting for the police to do anything. Will you come with us, Charles? It will be a terrific adventure."

" That would be marvellous," he said slowly, " but I can't come. I gave my word to the sergeant at the police station to go back and I promised Uncle faithfully I'd go back to Manlands this morning. He was quite decent last night and says that he's got something important to tell me. And there's that letter from Mother waiting for me, too. . . . I couldn't break my word to him now."

" Not even to get the fiddle back and be in the Albert Hall to-morrow evening? " Juliet asked, feeling rather mean.

" I can't break my word," Charles said stubbornly, " but I will ask him if I can go and I will make him go after the police about Bland and Foxy. You're sure it was them, I suppose? "

Juliet turned her back on him to greet her father and Mr. Messenger.

" Charles can't come with us, Daddy. He's promised

to go home. . . . I've just thought of something, though. Do you remember, Simon, that when we heard Bland on the telephone—when we were in the dark outside —he said something about Chelsea and contacting somebody there? . . . Well, I think that proves that he's on his way to London, doesn't it? . . . Do please *hurry,* dear Father."

Mr. Buckingham shook hands with Mr. Messenger and put his hand on Charles' shoulder.

" That's all right, my lad. Don't you break your word once you've given it. Get up to the police station now and tell them we've seen Bland and the other chap driving east. Get in touch with your uncle and persuade him to persuade them to do something quickly, because this is really his business, not ours. If we get as far as London—I doubt if we've got enough petrol—and if you can come on to-morrow, enquire for us at 26, Luton Square, Chelsea. My brother lives there and we shall be staying with him, if we get as far. . . . Now then, kids, pack in."

They said good-bye to the Messengers first, then Juliet turned to Charles.

" Sorry if I was rude about coming. Didn't mean to be. . . . See you in London to-morrow I hope."

She turned and waved from the window as the Buckingham's ancient vehicle roared into palpitating life and took the road to Ross, Gloucester and the east.

Juliet leaned back and looked at the back of her father's head affectionately.

" Breakfast? " Simon murmured. " We haven't had any ! "

CHAPTER 10

CHARLES ON THE TRAIL

As soon as the Buckinghams drove off Charles, feeling utterly miserable, turned back into the cottage where Mrs. Messenger, with concern in her kindly face, took his arm and led him back to the kitchen.

"I cannot make head nor tail of what's going on round here last night and this morning, what with policemen and nice gentlemen like the father of those two youngsters. But you, my lad, can do with a cup o' tea and some breakfast. Come and sit down."

"And if it helps at all to speak out then tell us your worries," said the silver-haired verger. "We trust you, lad. We know you've done nothing wrong."

Charles had found a lot of unexpected kindness during the last few days and it was some moments now before he could trust his voice to answer.

"You are very kind to me. There isn't really very much to say, except that I was unhappy in my uncle's home—I haven't got a father—and that I ran off to try and earn my own way for a few weeks. Uncle got the police to find me and after I've been up to see the sergeant again I've got to cycle home and it's rather a rotten finish to a grand two days with my new friends."

He went on to tell them a little about the stolen violin, but it all sounded rather unlikely and complicated and he was quite relieved when Mr. Messenger got up and said:

"Keep your promises, boy, and do your duty. . . .

Now I must be off to mine. Come and see us again
when you're in Hereford and bring your fiddle with you.
. . . We're always glad to welcome any who can make
music," and then, rather unexpectedly, " God bless you,
my lad! 'Tis a pity you've no time to come into the
Cathedral now."

Charles shook hands with them both, thanked them
again and wheeled his bicycle up towards the police
station. In spite of the promise he had made over the
telephone to his uncle last night he still felt bitter because he could not go after Bland and Foxy himself. It
was not that he did not trust the Buckinghams but it
was, after all, his own precious violin that they were
chasing and one glance at the car which Juliet and Simon
described rather grandly as " the vehicle," suggested that
it would have a poor chance of catching anything which
Mr. Bland would own! And the more he thought about
it, the more unreasonable did his Uncle Martin seem by
making him return to the police. And then cycling all
the way back to Manlands made him look a fine fool.
Juliet had thought so, anyway, and as he remembered
her words to him in the Messengers' kitchen last night he
smiled ruefully. Those two were lucky to have such
wonderful parents and he was sure that not many fathers
would have entered into this particular adventure so
enthusiastically. Then he remembered the letter from
his mother waiting for him at Manlands and decided to
ask Hetty to read it to him over the telephone before
he spoke to his uncle.

He was greeted kindly at the police station by the
sergeant who allowed him to use the telephone, but who
seemed very reluctant to say anything about the stolen
violin.

" But I do promise you, sergeant, that my friends saw
him driving his car over the bridge at eight o'clock this
morning," he explained. " The man Simmonds, who
stole the violin from the caravan, was sitting in the
back. . . . My friends and their father have gone after
him anyway."

" They have, have they? Doing the work of the police
for them. Very kind I must say. Most considerate and
helpful. . . . Septimus Bland of Maryknoll near Ludlow
you said was the name of the party, didn't you? . . .
Ah yes. Thank you. . . . If you want the telephone now
you'd better take it. . . . Tell Mr. Strong that you're
safe and sound and on your way home."

Hetty answered the telephone.

" This is Charles, Hetty! I'm grand, thanks, and had
some wonderful adventures, but I'm coming home this
morning. Where's Cyril and Derek? . . . Out for the
day? Good. . . . I say, Hetty, be a sport. Uncle told
me that a letter has come for me from Mother. Can
you find it and read it to me? . . . On the hall table?
All right I'll hold on while you fetch it. . . . I don't
know what I'd do without you, Hetty. . . . Got it?
Good. . . . Where's Uncle 'cos I'll have to speak to him
in a minute. . . . Open it quickly, Hetty darling and
read it. . . ."

Thin but clear, her dear old voice came over the wire
bringing him the most wonderful news.

" ' I am coming home at once, Charles dear,' " she read,
" ' and you will be surprised to see how much better I
am. I have other exciting news for you also, for your
father's violin concerto is to be performed for the first
time in England at the Albert Hall in London on Saturday next and will be conducted by Sir Harold Coatbridge.

You must be there, Charles, and I have written to Uncle Martin to explain and asked him to give you enough money for your journey. I cannot get to London until an hour or so before the performance, so you must meet me at the Albert Hall. Special seats will be arranged for us but you must go to the secretary's office and say who you are. If I am not there they will show you to Loggia No. 13, which they have promised will be reserved for us. I am longing to see you, my dear boy. Remember to come dressed as respectably as possible for once. . . . God bless you. . . . Till Saturday, Your loving Mother.' . . . There you are, Master Charles. I told you that you'd have good news as soon as you ran off, didn't I? . . . All right, my boy. . . . Don't carry on like that. I've read you every word that's down here in black and white in your mother's own dear writing. . . . Of course it's true. . . . Stop fussing and come home as quick as you can. Mr. Strong was telling me that you're at a police station, but I can't rightly believe that. . . . Speak to your uncle? Of course you can. He's in his study now." . . .

Charles waited for Mr. Strong without caring very much what sort of reception he was going to get. Nothing mattered much now that his mother was coming home and that they would meet at the Albert Hall to-morrow.

"Good morning, my boy," came his uncle's voice. "You are at the police station I presume. I was about to leave a message there for you as I have heard from your mother. . . . I beg your pardon? . . . I see! Hetty read your own letter to you over the telephone. . . . Good! Can you go to-morrow? Of course you can. I understand that some music composed by your father is to be performed for the first time, so of course you must be there. . . . Stay where you are now. I will come over in the car and fetch you as soon as I can."

" But Uncle," Charles gasped in surprise, " That's grand of you, but I want to get on to London to-day if I can and catch up my friends. . . . I told you last night about the violin being stolen. Juliet and Simon and their father are chasing a man called Bland now. We're sure he's got the fiddle but nothing I can say will make the police here believe me."

" Wait at the police station," Mr. Strong ordered in a very firm, business voice. " I'll come as quickly as I can," and rang off.

Charles replaced the receiver, sat back, and smiled broadly at the sergeant.

" Did you hear that? He's coming to fetch me in the car. I shan't have to cycle, and I can tell you that when he does arrive he'll get things moving. I'm going to the Cathedral for an hour but don't worry—I'll be back," and he strolled out into the sunshine.

He found Mr. Messenger about his duties in the Cathedral and after giving him the good news spent a happy hour in his company, exploring the Cathedral, listening to stories about it and then sitting in the choir stalls while the organist practised. While he rested there in peace he was puzzled by his uncle's changed mood. The more he considered it the more remarkable it seemed until he began to wonder if he were trying to hide something from him. The only news which is worth hiding at all is usually bad news, and for a few minutes he worried himself by wondering whether anything terrible had happened and that his uncle was driving over to break some bad news.

He was waiting on the steps of the police station when

Mr. Strong drove up. Almost before he had stopped Charles opened the door and said, " You haven't any bad news for me, have you sir? I had a stupid idea that you might have."

Mr. Strong gave him a queer look.

" No, Charles. No bad news. Don't worry. Hetty has packed up some decent clothes for you and here's your mother's letter, but there's no time to read it now. . . . Come and tell your story of this mysterious Mr. Bland to the sergeant again while I'm with you."

But this time there was another man with the sergeant—a man not in uniform, who was obviously a detective and who listened sympathetically to Charles and asked quick and intelligent questions. Charles told his story well but was aware that his uncle, sitting on a hard chair beside him, kept watching him in an unusual and almost kindly way. When the boy had finished Mr. Strong got up and put a hand on his shoulder and glanced meaningly at the detective.

" If you will just leave us alone for a few minutes, Charles, I should like a private word with these gentlemen. . . . May he wait outside, sergeant, if there is nothing else you wish to ask him? "

Charles kicked his heels on the pavement, wondering whatever he had done to make his uncle so amiable. He had expected anger, sarcasm and cold recrimination, but although he could not have expressed the new mood in words it suggested a renewed interest, and if not compassion, almost affection. It was very odd and Charles, who did not like anything he could not explain, was uneasy and unhappy about it even while re-reading his mother's letter, which Mr. Strong had brought.

When Mr. Strong reappeared he was looking very

serious and stood for a long minute on the steps of the police station looking out into the street over Charles' head. At last he spoke. " You told your story well, Charles. . . . A very remarkable story indeed. . . . I can hardly believe that Septimus Bland. . . ."

" They believe me now, don't they Uncle? I'm sure they didn't last night and I must have my fiddle back. You do see that, don't you? "

" I do indeed, my boy. It is more than ever important that the violin is recovered. The police will do everything now. You can rest assured of that," and, quite unexpectedly he smiled at him.

" What I'd like to do now sir, if you don't mind, is go off to London on my own—Mr. Buckingham gave me an address in Chelsea where they'll be—26, Luton Square. His brother lives there, and I would like to get there to-night in case they've arrived and have got any news, and then to-morrow I could explore and go and look at the Albert Hall from outside and have some fun. . . . Do you mind if I do that? "

He did not dare suggest that his uncle take him in the car to London but he was certainly surprised when Mr. Strong nodded his agreement.

" Very well, Charles. I think you might do that. Go in and give the detective that address in Chelsea, just in case they want to get into touch with you, and tell him from me that you will go up on an afternoon train."

There were no difficulties about that and when he returned Mr. Strong was already in the driving seat with the engine running.

" Before we leave Hereford I should like you to take me to the verger's cottage. I wish to thank the good woman there for her hospitality to you."

" Mr. Buckingham did that, sir, and I've thanked them several times—"

" Don't argue, boy. Do as I ask you," and as this was very much more like the normal Martin Strong, Charles did as he was told and waited in the car, while Mrs. Messenger was interviewed once again. When Mr. Strong came out he was smiling broadly.

" You seem to have made some very original friends, Charles. You must tell me more about them."

He turned the car and rather to Charles' surprise took the Worcester road.

" Where are we going, sir? Did you say I was to go on an afternoon train? "

" I must go to my office in Birmingham. The London trains from there are very much better and it would not be very wise if you arrived as a stranger at Luton Square before your friends. Clean clothes are in that suitcase at the back so there is no need for us to go back to Manlands. You can change at my office and if time hangs heavily on your hands you might even visit the cinema. How does that suit you? "

Charles was so astonished at being asked such a question that all he could say was, " Thank you very much, sir. That will be grand."

The journey to Birmingham was not very exciting and Charles' rather uneasy attempts at conversation were received without much enthusiasm, although his uncle's underlying kindness and interest were still obvious. Even when he reminded his uncle that he had left his bicycle at the police station Mr. Strong did not seem particularly disturbed and the nearer they got to Birmingham the more unreal to Charles did the journey become. He thought a lot about the Buckinghams and wondered how they were progressing. Much as he liked them he still felt a little humiliated at the way in which they had taken over the responsibility for finding his fiddle. But perhaps the police would really do something now, and in any case it would be wonderful if they could all meet in London.

Mr. Strong's offices were as austere and efficient looking as their owner and Charles, as he followed his uncle upstairs to a dim room with a red carpet and mahogany panelled walls, felt as if he ought to remove his shoes because he was on holy ground!

He washed and changed in a tiny cloakroom and was then taken out to lunch. Only once did Mr. Strong refer to the past when he looked over his coffee cup at his nephew and said, a little hesitantly:

" I hope you have not always been unhappy at Manlands, Charles? "

" No sir! I have been very happy most of the time. . . . I'm sorry about that scrap up with Derek and Cyril. I think I'll feel better about everything now that Mother is coming back."

" I think you will, my boy. You will find everything quite different I am sure," and with this cryptic remark he paid his bill and led the way out of the restaurant. He said no more until they were back at his office when, to Charles' astonishment, he presented him with four one pound notes.

" As you are so keen to go to London to-night I am not going to oppose you, Charles. We must remember, however, that neither of us knows anything about Mr. Buckingham's brother in Chelsea—from what you tell me his address was only thrown to you in a casual remark—so if the gentleman does not exist or you cannot

meet your somewhat eccentric friends, you must go to
the address on this card. This lady is a cousin of your
aunt's and has a small hotel in Kensington. I shall telephone her and ask her to find you a bed if you need
one. . . . I suggest that you go to the cinema now and
catch the 4.45 to Paddington from Snow Hill. It will
be more sensible for you to arrive in London after your
friends and not before. . . . Good-bye, my boy, and the
very best of luck to you to-morrow. Do not worry too
much about the violin, and I wish you to give your
mother a special message from me as soon as you see
her."

He took off his spectacles, polished them violently and
then continued in a slightly husky voice, " Give her
my love and wish her every possible happiness," and
with these astonishing words he shook hands, gave
Charles his suitcase and pushed him out of the room.

Charles found a cinema and sat and dozed in the
dark for a few hours without taking very much notice
of the film. He was still dazed by the turn of events,
his uncle's strange behaviour and the strong feeling that
something was going to happen—something which
others knew about but which was being kept from him.
Yesterday's journey in the sunshine from Ludlow to
Hereford seemed a distant dream as did the adventure
at the fair. Everything was different and—odd.

But Snow Hill station was normal enough and he
bought a cup of tea and a bun while waiting for the
express to come in. The journey was uneventful until
they reached High Wycombe. He had bought a magazine, but this strange, persistent feeling of uneasy
excitement prevented him from reading and he had
hardly looked up when the train had stopped at

Leamington Spa. But that was over an hour ago and
when he glanced at his watch as the brakes were applied
he saw that the time was nearly half-past six. Idly he
yawned and stretched and then went into the corridor
and looked out of the window as the train stopped.
And it was just forty seconds later that his rather dream-
like day vanished in a sudden shock of reality for,
glancing back down the train, he noticed a slight commotion round the stairs. A man, carrying a violin case,
was pushing his way through the people making for the
exit, and with a gasp of excitement Charles recognized
Mr. Bland, although there was no sign of Foxy. The
guard was already waving his flag and shouted a warning as the man scrambled into a carriage and Charles
went back to his own compartment.

What should he do? Suppose Bland came along the
corridor and recognized him? He huddled back in the
farthest corner and covered his face with the magazine
just in case of such an eventuality and then remembered
that Bland would certainly not be expecting to see him!
Then he wondered whether there was any way in which
he could recover the violin at once? Whether by some
trick Bland could be persuaded to leave his compartment
without taking the violin with him? Charles doubted
this and was still puzzling over the reason for his enemy's
appearance at High Wycombe when the train roared
through Denham and he realized that he would soon
have to decide what he was going to do. Should he,
for instance, find the guard and tell him that the police
were looking for Bland? Should he wait until he got
to Paddington, look for a policeman and risk missing
the wanted man? Then he remembered that Bland himself had spoken about meeting someone in Chelsea.

N

Surely it would be more sensible to follow him at Paddington and try to find out where he was going? Once he had been run to earth he could go to the nearest police station, or to 26, Luton Square, where he hoped to find the Buckinghams.

Charles grinned to himself as the train slid through Ealing Broadway. He was on the trail at last and if he had found Bland there was little doubt that the Buckinghams had lost him, and there was a certain amount of satisfaction in this selfish thought. Then he remembered that the road along which Bland would travel to London would almost certainly go through Oxford and High Wycombe, and his sudden appearance at the station might not, after all, be such a coincidence. It was quite possible for a car to break down, and quite possible for Simon to puncture a car's tyres—if the Buckinghams had ever caught up with their victim.

He jumped up and reached for his case as the train rattled over the points outside the terminus, and a few minutes later he was on the platform, sniffing the fishy smell that was his first memory of Paddington. His heart was banging excitedly as he hid behind a pile of luggage and watched for his victim.

Then he saw Bland, looking extremely pleased with himself, as he bustled down the platform with the stolen violin towards the queue of waiting taxis. He followed as closely as possible but could not get near enough to hear the address which he gave to his driver but as he drove off Charles, who was not at all used to London taxis, plucked up his courage and ran up to the next cab.

" I know it sounds like a detective story," he said with his disarming smile, " but please help me. I came to

Then he saw Bland, looking extremely pleased with himself. . . .

meet that man in the taxi in front but he wasn't expecting me and I couldn't catch him up. I've got an important message for him. Please follow his cab. I think he's going to Chelsea. . . . I've got plenty of money. I can pay."

The man looked at him and winked.

"Jump in, son. It's your money I'm after."

Charles was not very familiar with London but did soon realize that he had found another friend in his driver who managed to keep Bland's taxi in sight. Past Marble Arch they went, through the Park, round Hyde Park Corner, where they almost lost him, round

Sloane Square and into King's Road. They were, perhaps, a hundred yards behind the leading taxi when it turned sharp left, and by the time they were round the corner themselves their quarry was getting out opposite a big block of modern flats.

" Please don't stop," Charles said as he opened the window. " I want to surprise him. Just go past and then turn back."

The driver did as he was asked and then, as the other taxi drove off, Charles waited until Mr. Bland had gone in. He was feeling rather panicky and wondering what to do next when, " Come on, mate," the driver said cheerfully. " Wot yer going ter do? Get aht or stay in? "

Charles got out.

" Here's five shillings," he said. " Will you please wait? I promise I won't be long," and he ran into the hall of the flats before he lost his courage.

The porter looked at him enquiringly.

" A gentleman came in just now and if he was carrying a violin and his name is Mr. Bland I've got a message for him. What is the number of his flat, please? "

" Mr. Ruffle 'as just come in, son, and I reckon it was a fiddle 'e was carrying. Very musical is Mr. Ruffle, but 'e's not so often 'ere. Lives in country up in Midlands 'e told me once. No. 139, sixth floor."

" Thank you very much indeed. Maybe I've made a mistake," Charles said and ran out to the waiting taxi.

He had done it! The fox was now safely in his earth and he was the only one of the hounds who knew where it was.

" Where to now, me lord? " said the taxi driver, who seemed thoroughly amused. " Buckingham Palace? "

Charles laughed.

" Take me to 26, Luton Square, Chelsea. . . . No, wait! To the Albert Hall first, please. I want to see the posters."

CHAPTER II

PURSUIT

THE Buckinghams had no illusions left about their
ancient car. None of them was mechanically minded,
and Mr. Buckingham's expression of resignation when
" the vehicle " refused to start on a cold morning or
stopped on a hill was something which his family now
accepted in preference to the much rarer outbursts of
baffled rage to which they had occasionally been wit-
nesses. But they had, nevertheless, a real affection for
the old warrior, and as Mr. Buckingham guided her
over Hereford's lovely Wye Bridge on this bright Friday
morning Simon, sitting in the front, said, " I hope she's
in good training, Daddy? " and his father understood
him.

Juliet, on the back seat, forbore to ask whether he
had brought his petrol coupons and merely quoted,
rather inaptly, " *If you have tears prepare to shed them
now.*"

" This ridiculous escapade," Mr. Buckingham said,
" is probably the craziest thing I have ever done in a
blameless, though misguided, career. Can either of you
describe the car we are supposed to be chasing? "

" Certainly," Juliet said. " Long, low and black."

" That makes it all very much easier. Did you see
the number or could you recognize the make? "

Juliet wrinkled her forehead. " It wasn't a Rolls
Royce. That's all I'm sure about."

" You both realize that we may be obstructing the

198

course of justice or at least doing something which is
the duty of the police? We are certainly not minding
our own business."

"We don't think much of the police," Simon said,
"and I don't see why you shouldn't take us for a drive
towards London. We're not doing anything actually
criminal, are we? "

But Juliet, before her father could answer, said in the
small voice of a temptress, "We did think that there
might be an idea for a story for you in all this, Daddy
darling. . . . And besides, we do want to help Charles.
If we do catch Mr. Bland I'll go right up and ask him
for the fiddle. I'm not afraid of him and I honestly
think he'd hand it over."

Soon after they reached the outskirts of Gloucester.

"We're seeing a lot of cathedrals lately," Simon remarked. "I shouldn't think Mr. Bland would stop to
go into a cathedral."

"Maybe that's just where you're wrong, little man,"
Juliet explained. "Bland spends most of his time pretending to be Septimus Bland the musician. He may
not be feeling that way just now, of course, but he might
easily be in the cathedral right now listening to the
music with his hands together. Don't you think he might,
Daddy? "

"Don't ask me questions like that until I'm through
this city. . . . Something seems to tell me that the vehicle
is faltering slightly."

"Petrol, darling! Have you petrol in her? "

"I shouldn't think so. How much easier life with
the vehicle would be if the petrol gauge worked," but
he stopped at the first petrol station once they were
clear of the city.

Juliet saw an uneasy expression cross his face as he paid for the petrol and passed over the coupons and her forebodings were justified when he said, " I must confess to my two confederates. We have barely enough petrol to reach London and none to get back. Every mile on now means that we may well be stranded far from home on our return. . . . I have, I fear, been a trifle improvident with my coupons this summer, but of course I did not expect to have to do this sort of thing. . . . Now what shall we do? Turn back now and hand over the whole problem to the police, or go on and run the risk of being stranded? "

" Go on, of course," they shouted and Simon, the practical, added, " You'll always get your petrol back from the police when they know how we've been helping them."

" A bright boy," Mr. Buckingham said as he let in the clutch, " but fairly soon now we shall have to start some sleuthing. There must be ways of finding out whether your Mr. Bland is in front of us. What would be his most likely reasons for stopping? "

" Petrol, a drink or a meal," Juliet said promptly.

" If we could only be sure that he is on the way to London I wouldn't be so worried," Mr. Buckingham admitted. " It's just that this is all guess work. It's no use making enquiries in Cheltenham, anyway and we're there now."

Six miles farther on they found the first clue. At the junction of two roads an R.A.C. scout was just locking a telephone box. Mr. Buckingham stopped and smiled.

" Can I help you, sir? "

" Oh, I do hope so," Juliet began, and then faltered at her father's glare.

"What I'm going to ask you sounds crazy, but if you've come from Oxford and are observant and have a good memory you may be able to help," and then and there Mr. Buckingham told a shameless story of a petrol lighter, much valued for sentimental reasons, which he had lent to two men in a Gloucester hotel and which must have been pocketed by one of them by mistake when they went out to their car.

"It was stupid of me but I didn't realize it until after they had gone. I've an idea that they were on their way to London, but I can't describe the car. Can you, Juliet?"

"New, I think, and long and low and black. I know that sounds feeble but that's all I can tell you. The man driving it was plump and rather pleasant-looking—like Mr. Pickwick—" at this the R.A.C. scout's face brightened, "and the man who was with him was in black and sandy-looking, with rimless spectacles."

"I'm a lover of Dickens myself, miss, but I've seen no one like that this morning though I've come from Oxford. I would have remembered him, but you'll understand that most of the cars I've seen to-day have been long and low and black."

"The other chap was rather foxy-looking," Simon said almost pleadingly. "He wasn't driving. Sitting in the back."

The scout put his finger to his nose and rubbed it reflectively.

"Foxy?" he murmured. "I wonder?" . . . Then, "Come to think of it I did see a miserable-looking chap in black sitting outside the 'Golden Cross' in Burford, drinking a glass o' beer. But I don't recollect the car, nor Mr. Pickwick. . . . But maybe a car was standing

outside. It must have been, but I do remember that the
bloke didn't look like the country, if you know what
I mean, sir. More like an undertaker. . . . I'm sorry I
can't help more but I hope you get your lighter back.
Good day, sir, and thank you."

"That's him all right," Simon said as they moved
off. "That's the miserable, skulking foxy-face. The
moment that man said he was like an undertaker I was
sure. That's how he would look. . . . Come on, Father!
We're hot on the trail."

"I can only hope that I shall be forgiven for that
shameful tissue of lies," Mr. Buckingham groaned. "I
attribute such an exhibition entirely to the influence of
my children. . . . We will eat, drink and enquire at the
'Golden Cross.'"

They drove on through the glory of the Cotswolds
with Mr. Buckingham rather unhappy about the vehicle,
which was now smelling strongly of petrol and very hot.
He had a sneaking suspicion that he had not filled up
with water, and as he knew from previous experience
that there was a slight, but dangerous, leak in that vital
part, he was looking forward, for more than one reason,
to the "Golden Cross."

They arrived twenty minutes later.

"Now she must rest," said Mr. Buckingham as he
got out and opened the bonnet, "and so must I. We
are both hot. Stay here, children, and I will bring you
out some sandwiches and ginger beer. . . . Simon! You
may wander round the back and make friends with someone in your inimitable way and bring a can of cold
water for the vehicle. . . . Do *not* touch the radiator
cap for about ten minutes. It's practically red hot."

The host of the "Golden Cross" confirmed that

Mr. Bland had been there an hour before as soon as he was given the reference to Mr. Pickwick.

" A pleasant enough gent, sir," he said. " No. I didn't notice his car, though he did remark that it was fairly new and that he was having some trouble with it. . . . Somebody else with him? No, sir. Not in here. . . . Come to think of it though he did say something about ' my man outside,' and took him out a glass of beer."

" He borrowed my lighter in the hotel in Gloucester and forgot to return it and I'd like to catch him if I can. Did he say he was going to London? "

" I don't think so, sir. . . . Sandwiches and ginger beer? Certainly."

" Yes. We're on the trail, family," Mr. Buckingham said as he joined his children on a bench outside, " but he's over an hour ahead although I don't think his car is going very well."

Juliet was all for rushing on at once and eating on the way, but her father told her that she must realize that they would never catch Bland on the road although they could at least follow his trail and contact the police later.

" And I must ring up your mother soon," he went on. " With very good reason she'll soon know that we've all taken leave of our senses, but if we do get as far as London we can all stay with Uncle Joe in Chelsea."

Juliet gulped her ginger beer and looked at her father affectionately.

" You think you're being all cool and calculating about this but really you'd love to catch Bland, wouldn't you, Daddy? You'd love to commandeer the first slinky, long-bonneted car that comes along and dash after him. I

know you would. So would I. So would little Simon
here. If you knew how Bland had patronized us and
called me ' young lady ' and then pushed us off when
he just wanted Charles on his own you'd be mad too."

" As for Foxy," Simon added, " he's the lowest thing
that crawls. I wish I could have seen his face when he
realized that I'd taken the valves out of his tyres! Do
you think we could stop the first really fast car that
comes along and ask for a lift? "

Mr. Buckingham did not think it wise to get anyone
else implicated in an unofficial pusuit of two likely
criminals and so, now that the vehicle had also had
some refreshment and cooled down, they went on their
way.

They had by-passed Oxford when an A.A. scout gave
them the encouraging news that their quarry was having
trouble with his car.

" These new cars must be run in, sir, and I reckon
the gent was pushing it hard. Will you be able to catch
him up? " The scout looked at the vehicle politely but
doubtfully. " Well, sir! You'd better not push this one
too hard either," and the two men smiled at each other
understandingly.

" I suppose there's a chance now," Mr. Buckingham
said as they started again, " but we can't have much
petrol left. I'm not going to hurry and I'm going to have
a cup of tea. . . . I've just remembered that somewhere
about here there's a side turning leading to a magnificent
and most enterprising road house called ' The Saucy
Kate.' Now if I was Mr. Septimus Bland at this time
of the afternoon I should want a cup of tea very badly
and if, as I suspect, he knows this road well, he will
also know ' The Saucy Kate.' . . . Something seems to

tell me, my children, that my wonderful instinct is at work again. . . . Keep a look out for a sign suggesting that we fork to the left."

Simon, who was now sitting in the back with his sister, saw it first.

" I was right, you see," his father said as he slowed down for the turn. " It is before you come to Wycombe and that's worth remembering. . . . Something seems to tell me." . . .

" We know, darling, but we shall lose hours if your something is telling you the wrong thing. But I'd like some tea too."

A few minutes later Simon gave a sort of strangled squeak.

" Go slowly! Be ready to stop. I think that man walking towards us is Foxy. . . . Look, Julie! "

Juliet peered over her father's shoulder.

About three hundred yards ahead of them a man in a black suit was trudging towards them along the white, dusty road. Mr. Buckingham slowed down. " If it is your Foxy friend he mustn't see you two. Get down in the back. What do you think, Julie? "

" Yes. I'm sure of it. What marvellous luck! I bet they've broken down and Foxy has been told to walk back to Ludlow. . . . Look! He's signalling us to stop! He wants a lift. How marvellous! Get down here, Simon. He mustn't see us. . . . Deal with him, Daddy."

Foxy approached with lagging feet. His black boots were white with dust, his face wet with perspiration, and when he removed his hat his forehead was marked with a red band. There was a flicker of contempt in his shifty eyes as he glanced at the vehicle and then, as he looked at Mr. Buckingham, his face went blank.

Foxy approached with lagging feet. His black boots
were white with dust.

"Thank you, sir. I am obliged to you for stopping,
but we need help urgently. My master's car has broken
down a mile beyond the road house, and as he is most
anxious to get to London at once it is imperative that
we obtain assistance. . . . It would be a kindness if you
could take me back to the nearest telephone. . . . The
instrument at ' The Saucy Kate ' is regrettably out of
order." He spoke the last few words through clenched
teeth.

"Very unfortunate for your master. Is he waiting in
the car?"

"Yes, sir. Perhaps you could give us a lift to London
yourself sir?"

"Perhaps I could. What is your master's name, by

the way, so that I can address him courteously when we meet? "

" Bland, sir. But if you could give us a lift perhaps I may return with you now? It has been a long walk and excessively dusty."

Mr. Buckingham laughed triumphantly.

" Out of my way," he said. " You're well named ' Foxy.' Just keep on walking."

With a whoop of joy Juliet and Simon popped up from the back and as the vehicle shot forward they saluted him with signs of derision and left him dancing in the road with rage.

After this events moved very quickly. The vehicle rattled past " The Saucy Kate " without a mention of tea from the excited hunters and soon after they found the long, low, black car by the roadside. Mr. Buckingham hooted and pulled up behind it and, signing to his children to remain in the background, approached with caution. The car was empty but there was a note on the steering wheel.

" *Simmonds. Have taken a lift and am going on by train. When car is repaired follow me to Chelsea. Telephone me in any case later. S.B.*"

Mr. Buckingham pocketed the note and dashed back to the vehicle.

" High Wycombe Station," he gasped. " I only hope the petrol lasts."

It did not. The vehicle gasped and choked into silence about three hundred yards from the station. The London train was coming in as they deserted the car, and going out as Simon and Juliet, yards ahead of their exhausted father, staggered into the booking hall.

" Yes," the ticket collector agreed, " there was

a plumpish gent with a fiddle just caught the London train. He come up in a butcher's van, miss, and gave the bloke a quid."

As soon as their father heard the news he led them to a nearby garage.

" My car, down the street, has run out of petrol, and I have no more coupons. Please take it in and look after it. . . . Now I want to hire another car with a driver to take us to the nearest station that has a train to Paddington. And I'm in a hurry."

People ran to his bidding while Juliet and Simon stood by silent with admiration. The car took them to Slough and they had to wait only a few minutes for a train.

At Paddington Mr. Buckingham strode towards the line of waiting taxis with his children, faint but pursuing, in the rear.

" This is wonderful and most exciting," Juliet gasped, "but what do we do now? London's a big place to search."

" You're getting dull, my child. Chelsea he said in the note he left for Foxy. And Uncle Joe lives in Chelsea. . . . 26, Luton Square, please driver."

Juliet and Simon were now in a kind of trance and barely noticed the journey across London. It was years since they had visited their Uncle Joe in London and although they were very fond of him they were too weary to notice the warmth of his welcome, or that he did not seem altogether surprised to see them.

" Go straight up to the studio, Julie," he said. " You'll be interested in something up there and I want to have a quiet word with your father."

She remembered the long, lofty studio with big

windows and bright cushions, but when she pushed open the door, with Simon at her heels, she almost fell backwards when she saw Charles grinning at them from the hearthrug.

" Hullo! I've beaten you to it, but I'm jolly glad to see you. . . . Listen, you two. I've found him. Bland I mean. He got on the train I was in and I followed him across London. He's in 139, Waverley Court, not far from here. He calls himself Ruffle and he's still got my fiddle. I didn't think I ought to go and get it on my own but now you've come we might as well do it together. Shall we go now? "

Juliet collapsed on to the orange cushions of the divan.

" You got here first, Charles, you beast! I can't think how you did it, but Daddy's used up all his petrol trying to help you."

Simon looked round suspiciously.

" You haven't brought that uncle of yours, have you? "

Charles grinned.

" No I haven't. But I found yours first! "

CHAPTER 12

CONCERTO

EACH morning since she had left Leasend, Juliet had wakened in a different bed, but the Saturday morning of the Renislau concert was the strangest wakening of all for she found herself sunk in the cushions of the enormous divan in Uncle Joe's studio. This big room was dim because the curtains were drawn, but she knew as soon as she woke that it was late and, instinctively, that even if it were late she had not to worry. Muffled noises in the distance suggested that somebody was about and then, as she turned over and hugged her eiderdown closer, the murmur of London traffic came through the open window and she remembered where she was and all the adventures of the previous evening.

She sighed happily, settled on her back and went over everything all over again.

As soon as they had sorted themselves out in Uncle Joe's bachelor flat and got used to being with Charles again, the brothers Buckingham lit their pipes and retired for a council of war. Juliet smiled to herself as she remembered how they had come back ten minutes later and, rather shamefacedly, told them that this was a job for the grown-ups and the police, because it might be dangerous.

But it had not been so very dangerous after all, although it was certainly the most exciting event in the lives of any of the children who had little trouble in

persuading the two men that they intended coming to
Waverley Court with them.

Charles had been unexpectedly firm.

" I expect the police will catch up later and anyway
we can tell them all about it, but I've got to have my
fiddle and I want it to-night. I believe Bland will give
it up to the three of us if we go on our own, but it
might be better to have some grown-ups handy."

And so it was eventually arranged, and they went out
together and packed into a taxi and then into the tiny
lift at Waverley Court and stood, dry-mouthed with excitement, outside the door of No. 139. Simon's teeth
began to chatter and Juliet found herself gripping
Charles' arm as the latter whispered:

" I can hear voices. He's got someone there."

Then the Buckingham grown-ups pushed the three
children behind them and rang the bell.

" Stay out here until we give you the word," Uncle
Joe said. " We shall go straight in."

Mr. Bland opened the door. Not quite so bland as
usual and very annoyed when two strangers pushed him
firmly back into his own hall. As he protested, Juliet,
Charles and Simon followed, and when Mr. Bland
recognized them his face became very ugly indeed. After
that the sequence of events was rather muddled, but
Juliet remembered how they had all crowded into a little
sitting-room with a table by the window from which
you could look out across the roofs and spires of London. Standing by the table was a small man in heavy
horn-rimmed glasses, and wearing a garish tie which
suggested that he was an American citizen. The violin
case was open on the table beside him, as was a cheque
book. He had a pen in his hand and a cigar in his

mouth and his astonishment was ludicrous as Charles began to speak.

"I expect you are Mr. Rankin. My name is Charles Renislau and my father was Alex Renislau, the composer, and that violin on the table was his and now it belongs to me. It has been stolen from me by Mr. Bland who, I think, is trying to sell it to you. I can describe my violin to you precisely and tell you where my father's signature is scratched on it, and these two gentlemen who have come with me will tell you how I can prove who I am. My mother will be home from Switzerland to-morrow in time for the concert at the Albert Hall and she will tell you that this fiddle is mine, and so will my uncle who I could reach on the telephone. . . . We've followed this man here and I think we're only just in time."

There was a long moment's silence then Bland began to bluster. Juliet went over to the window and smiled at the bewildered Mr. Rankin. Charles glared at Bland, Simon edged about the room rather like a suspicious terrier and the two men, both looking rather like excited small boys themselves, stood grimly by the door. But Bland was beaten now and knew it as Mr. Rankin returned his pen to his pocket and drawled:

"Whether your name is Bland or Ruffle I'd be glad to hear what you have got to say. . . . No need to make up any more lies. I can see the answer in your face. . . . Lucky for me, maybe, that these youngsters came along, and now I'm proud to shake the hand of the son of Alex Renislau."

Juliet could not remember seeing Bland slip out of the room, but on their way back to Luton Square her father had said, " We let him go. It wasn't our business.

It's for the police to arrest him. We shall ring them
up, of course, but nothing was so important as getting
the fiddle back."

It was fun after that when they told Mr. Rankin the
story of Maryknoll and the chase from Hereford to London. He came back to the studio with them and they
had a wonderful picnic meal during which Charles
had played his violin. The American had been kind but
rather boring, Juliet remembered, and just then there was
a bang on the studio door and Uncle Joe—smiling,
tousled, and clad in the most wonderful dressing-gown
she had ever seen—came in with a cup of tea.

" Hullo, niece," he said. " You're growing up and
look very nice this morning. . . . Let's have some daylight on that blonde head of yours. I must paint you
one day."

Juliet smiled at him and almost purred with pleasure
as she sat up and sipped her tea.

" What's happening to-day, Uncle Joe? Besides the
concert to-night, I mean."

" We—your father and I—did a lot of telephoning
last night after the children had been tucked up. The
police have been told, so now it's up to them. . . . Then,
don't get too excited, but your mother is coming this
afternoon in time for the Albert Hall, and young Charles
has been on the telephone to that queer household of
his. . . . I'm going to Brighton for the week-end of
course. Nobody thinks of me, Juliet. I'm only the man
who lives here."

" You're a very nice uncle," she said, patting a cushion
beside her, " and I've made up my mind that we're
coming to London more often. . . . I'm not at all sure

that this isn't going to be the most wonderful day of my life."

And that was how the day started. For Charles it was even more exciting because his mother, too, was on the way to London, and so were his uncle, aunt and old Hetty; the violin was safe; the concert was to come; and he was united again with the jolliest friends he had ever met. He could never remember clearly how they spent the day, except that Simon went off to the Zoo with Mr. Buckingham and that he and Juliet went exploring London on buses.

The others arrived at tea-time. His uncle, looking rather out of place in the untidy studio, and his aunt, too, trying not to look as if she considered overyone else to be socially inferior. But they were both kind. Hetty, dressed in her marvellous best, hugged him unashamedly, looked Juliet and Simon up and down critically and then, deciding that they were good enough for her Charles, she hugged them too. Then Mrs. Buckingham, who kissed her husband, her children, her brother-in-law and Charles also, which surprised him very much. In the midst of the babel the telephone rang and when Mr. Buckingham came back he called for silence. " That was the police," he announced. " They've caught Bland at Southampton and they got Simmonds last night soon after we telephoned. . . . You kids must be more careful of the company you keep in future. Mr. Bland was not a very nice person and seems to have been a receiver of stolen valuables and art treasures. Rich Americans are his hobby."

But throughout all the fun Charles felt again that strange feeling of excitement and uncertainty. Every now and then he sensed that the grown-ups—particularly his uncle, aunt and Hetty—were watching him and felt that they were keeping something from him.

The party arrived at the Albert Hall in three taxis just after seven and Charles was thrilled to see the queues outside each of the entrances round the great, circular building, and all the posters bearing his father's name.

" You have to call at the secretary's office, haven't you, Charles? We will wait for you here," his uncle said.

Charles suddenly felt small and alone. Proud and excited, too, but this sense of mystery was something he had never experienced before.

Surely the commissionaire gave him a second, meaning glance when he asked for the secretary's office? For a moment he hesitated before the closed door and then a familiar voice behind him said, " Go on, Johnny! Get it over! I'll come in with you if you like—or would you rather I waited here? "

Just the sort of thing which Juliet would do, of course. To leave the others because she guessed how he was feeling.

" No. I wouldn't," he said gruffly. " Come in," and then, when a woman at a desk inside smiled enquiringly at them he said, a little too loudly because he was nervous, " My name is Charles Renislau. My mother asked me to call—"

As soon as they heard his name three other women at the back of the office looked up and then twittered together, but the one to whom he had spoken said, " We are all proud to know you are here. This is a great occasion for you, I'm sure. Here are tickets for Loggia No. 13. Mrs. Renislau will join you there and the rest of your party will be in the boxes next door. Everything has been arranged."

Still feeling completely dazed he thanked them and with Juliet at his side went out and joined the others. It may have been imagination or excitement, but he thought that all the grown-ups looked at him oddly.

His uncle led the way down a curving, stone-flagged corridor, now full of hurrying people. An attendant unlocked the doors of Loggias 14 and 15.

" You're in 13, Charles. Your mother will come there, but we shall be next door. . . . Good luck ! "

As No. 13 was unlocked in turn:

" Juliet and Simon with me, please," Charles said. " We've been through a lot together and I want them now."

" We shall go when your mother comes, Johnny— Charles, I mean—but it's nice of you to ask us. I should like to sit in the front for a bit. I don't suppose that you noticed but I washed my hair this afternoon and I don't see why I shouldn't show it off."

Temporarily, Simon seemed overwhelmed by the occasion, but they sat down together on three chairs in the front of the box, leaned their elbows on the ledge and looked down into the great, circular auditorium. Loggia No. 13 was at the back of about ten rows of sloping stalls and looked down into the famous " promenade," which was already thick with standing enthusiasts, and across it to the tiered platforms on to which the orchestra would soon file—drums and tympani on the right, horns on the left and the strings on each side of the conductor's rostrum. Above the orchestra were the pipes of the mighty organ and, when they looked higher still, above two more tiers of boxes, a gallery and an amphitheatre, they saw the great roof of aluminium.

Charles looked at his watch. Seven-fifteen and the auditorium was nearly full. He glanced to his right and smiled feebly at Mr. and Mrs. Buckingham in the next box, but he now felt too sick with excitement to trust his voice.

Juliet was speaking. " Charles. I feel absolutely awful. I suppose this is the most wonderful day in the whole of your life. . . . Look. Here's the programme. Your concerto is second—after the *Magic Flute Overture*. See? There's your father's name and it says ' First Performance in London.' "

" I know, Julie. It's almost too exciting. I never thought it would be as bad, but I do wish my mother would come."

At seven-twenty the lights above the orchestra went up and a few minutes later the musicians began to file in and tune up. At seven-twenty-five there was a burst of applause as the leader of the orchestra bowed and took his place; and at seven-twenty-six Charles felt his mother's hands on his shoulders and by the time he had turned to greet her Juliet and Simon had slipped out of the door and closed it behind them.

She drew him to the back of the box and kissed him. He had never known her look so well and happy and as she laughed at him the tears slipped down her face.

" I'm so sorry, darling," she gulped, " to be so late and to have been so mysterious about everything. Let me look at you. Are you as well as you look? "

" And you, Mother? Are you really all right now and not going back to Switzerland? Sure? "

" Your uncle and aunt are next door I suppose? Who were the two children in here? That girl with the lovely hair? "

" The best friends I've got, Mother. You'll meet them presently."

Another roar of applause heralded the conductor, Sir Harold Coatbridge, and in the few seconds' silence before the opening bars of Mozart's best known overture, Mrs. Renislau took her son's arm and whispered, " Come outside, Charles. I have something important to tell you."

The long corridor was empty except for a bored-looking attendant and as the music began his mother began to speak.

" What I am going to tell you, my dear, is difficult, although wonderful news. Only I can tell it you. I can trust you to be brave and sensible, can't I? . . . To be your father's son? "

He nodded. His heart was thudding almost in his throat. Now he was to hear the secret which others already knew.

" Can you see how happy I am, dear Charles? Can you see that life is going to start again for me as it is for you? Your father, Charles, is alive. He flew with me from Switzerland this afternoon. He has been an outlaw and a prisoner. He has been ill. He has escaped and been recaptured and escaped again, and one day you will hear the whole wonderful story. I have never admitted to myself that he was dead and many friends for many years in many countries have been searching for him, and not much more than a month ago a rumour came from Switzerland and so, although I dared not tell you then, I had to go—are you listening, Charles? It's true, my dear. Your father is alive. He is safe and fairly well and will be with us both now for always. In a few minutes he will walk on down there and conduct his own concerto. Sir Harold, who only met him an hour ago, insists. You will see your father take his rightful place, Charles. . . . He does not look so much changed but it must be difficult for you to remember him."

" Of course I remember him. I could never forget. I can't believe it even now, Mother."

" Look at me and you will know it is true. Forgive me breaking the news to you in this way. I did not want to write or telegraph. I would not have anyone else tell you, but I had to let your uncle know because he has always been good to me."

" I see," Charles said. " Now I understand why he has been so kind to me suddenly. You had told him about—Father," and he spoke the last word almost shyly. " I'd like to tell my friends now," and he opened the door of No. 14.

Juliet and Simon were standing just inside and as soon as they saw him Juliet turned to him impetuously and, making no attempt to check the tears streaming down her face, pulled Simon out after her and closed the door.

" They've told us, Charles. Your uncle told us. I don't know what to say, but you do know what Simon and the parents and I feel, don't you? You know we can't say how happy we are for you. I said just now that this was the most wonderful day of your life, didn't I? "

Charles found a shaky laugh.

" I've found my mother, too. . . . This is Juliet and Simon, Mother. . . . It seems silly just to say ' Thank you,' Julie, but I'm glad you're both here."

But Simon was still without words. His hair was tousled, his beaming face red and shining, but he was dumb.

Mrs. Renislau . . . stood behind her son with a hand on his shoulder.

The overture finished and during the applause the four of them went back to No. 13. Mrs. Renislau put Juliet and Simon in chairs next to Charles but stood behind her son with a hand on his shoulder.

Sir Harold came back to the rostrum, bowed to the great audience, held up his hand for silence.

"Ladies and gentlemen," he began as the murmur of astonishment died. "I have important news for you. Alex Renislau, the distinguished Polish composer, whose greatest work you are about to hear performed in Britain for the first time to-night, has not been heard of since the sack of Warsaw. Most of us have presumed him to have been killed in action—or worse.

' Ladies and gentlemen, Alex Renislau was not killed

in action, although one day the full story of his suffer-
ings and his heroism may be told. He landed in London
by air from Switzerland with his wife only a few hours
ago and I have, with great difficulty, persuaded him to
conduct his own concerto here and now—"

A roar of applause and cheers interrupted the great
conductor who bowed, smiled again and left the stage.
Three men in the back row of the stalls next to the
gangway a few feet away from them, jumped to their
feet and dashed for the exit and Juliet, with a thrill,
realized that they were newspaper reporters.

Then there was fresh applause as the famous soloist
took his place and then turned with all the orchestra
to the entrance of the narrow tunnel leading up to the
stage.

Then, in an unforgettable few seconds, Charles saw
the father whom he had believed to be dead. Slim and
straight he walked nervously into the glare of the lights
and stopped in surprise and embarrassment as the
audience began to cheer. His own father! Distinguished,
even though he was dressed in an old suit and a soft
collar. Nervous, as he twitched at his tie and then pushed
back the lock of hair which his son had inherited. He
turned and picked up the baton three times before they
would let him begin, but at last the audience settled
to attentive and excited silence.

Then came the lovely motif which Mr. Bland had
so unexpectedly known and which had become part
of Charles' own life. The first movement died away and
the second began ecstatically. Ten minutes from the end
Mrs. Renislau whispered:

" Come, Charles. It is time to go."

They walked a long way round the corridor until

they came to a pair of glass doors marked " Performers only." A strange man smiled at Mrs. Renislau, unexpectedly shook hands with Charles and let them through into a lobby. They turned to the right and another attendant, not in uniform, smiled another welcome and showed them into an old-fashioned room with three curtained alcoves, cream painted walls and a few chairs covered in blue plush.

" This is the room reserved for the chief artistes, Charles. We will wait here for your father. . . . Now here is Sir Harold. . . . My son, Charles, Sir Harold. Perhaps one day he will realize just how kind you have been to-night. I shall never forget it."

The great conductor shook hands with Charles and beamed at him and then the attendant put his head round the door.

" He's finished, sir, and the audience has gone mad."

Mrs. Renislau got up with shining eyes.

" I can't wait in here. Come, Charles."

She led him out into the lobby and pointed forward to the short, sloping passage which led up to the stage.

" We call that the Bull Run, son," the attendant said as he opened the glass door to let in a crash of applause. " Here comes the soloist! "

Three times the hot, but happy performer, went back to take his call and at last he too shook hands with Charles and his mother.

The applause, now mingled with cheers, crashed out again. Charles felt his mother's hands pushing him gently forwards. He heard Sir Harold murmur something behind him. He saw the attendant open the door again and smile at him encouragingly, and then he seemed to be suddenly alone, staring ahead along the Bull Run, while the applause beat rhythmically like the waves of the sea. Then he saw his father coming and took two, unsteady steps forward to meet him.

This is the first book about the Buckinghams and Charles Renislau. There are two more stories about them called, " The Buckinghams at Ravenswyke" and " The Long Passage."